THE DUKE UNDER THE MISTLETOE

A STEAMY CHRISTMAS NOVELLA

SCARLETT SCOTT

BLURB

Lillian: New York City socialite, wealthy heiress, and duchess against her will.

She didn't want to get married. Not yet. And certainly not to a cold, haughty aristocrat.

But her mother had other plans.

Now, she's a duchess about to spend Christmas alone at her new husband's crumbling country estate.

There's just one problem.

He's unexpectedly decided to join her.

Alaric: Impoverished duke, London's most eligible bachelor, and husband against his will.

He may descend from one of the noblest families in England, but he's swimming in a century's worth of debt.

His only hope was to secure a wealthy wife.

But his duty isn't over.

Because he needs an heir.

And there's only one way to get one…

The Duke Under the Mistletoe

All rights reserved.

Copyright © 2025 by Scarlett Scott™

Published by Happily Ever After Books, LLC

Edited by Grace Bradley and Lisa Hollett, Silently Correcting Your Grammar

Cover Design by Wicked Smart Designs

This book or any portion thereof may not be reproduced or used in any manner whatsoever without the express written permission of the publisher except for the use of brief quotations in a book review.

The unauthorized reproduction or distribution of this copyrighted work is illegal. No part of this book may be scanned, uploaded, or distributed via the Internet or any other means, electronic or print, without the publisher's permission. Criminal copyright infringement, including infringement without monetary gain, is punishable by law.

This book is a work of fiction and any resemblance to persons, living or dead, or places, events, or locales, is purely coincidental. The characters are productions of the author's imagination and used fictitiously.

Scarlett Scott™ is a registered trademark of Happily Ever After Books, LLC.

For more information, contact author Scarlett Scott™.

https://scarlettscottauthor.com/

For Isabell, Queen of Names

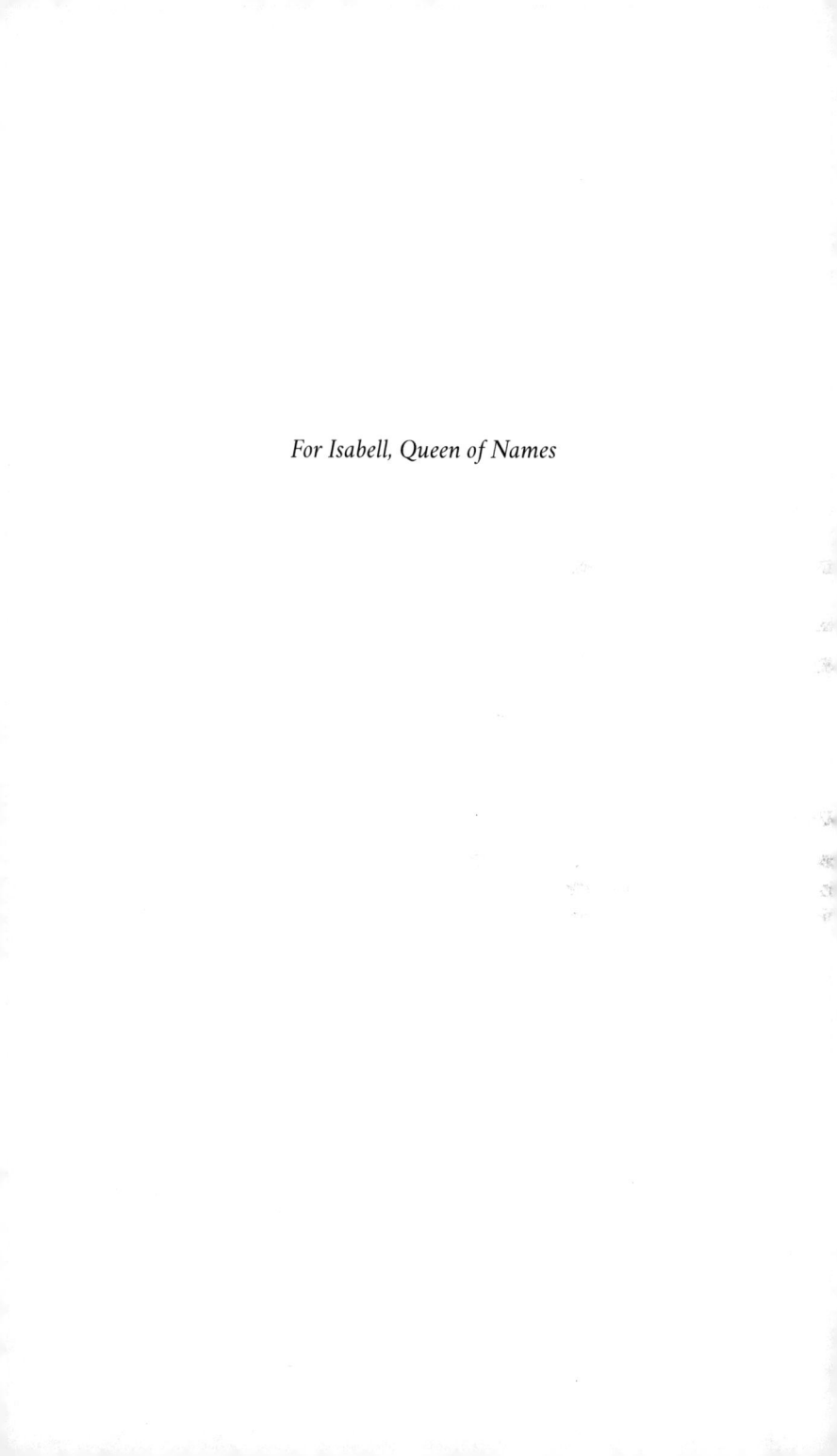

CHAPTER 1

ENGLAND 1889

"Is everything prepared to your liking, Your Grace?" asked Mrs. Greaves.

The Wentworth Abbey housekeeper's tone was stoic. To her credit, there was nary a hint of distaste in either her voice or her expressionless face. She wore a stern black gown, her steel-gray hair pulled tightly into a chignon, and the chatelaine at her waist likely weighed as much as one of the many portmanteaus Lillian had brought from New York City. The housekeeper looked rather as if she were dressed in mourning.

And perhaps she was.

After all, no one was happy that England's most-revered bachelor, the Duke of Wentworth, had married an American heiress.

Including the duke himself, as he had made more than apparent in word and deed, breaking her fragile hopes and burgeoning feelings into tiny shards in the process.

"I'm sure it is, Mrs. Greaves," Lillian returned politely.

They were ensconced in a sitting room that must have

been cheerful a century ago. Time and a marked lack of ducal funds had not been kind to it. The ceiling paint had peeled in abject decay. A large water spot in the shape of Pennsylvania marred the plaster below mullioned windows, the wall coverings had long ago faded, and the Axminster was threadbare.

On any number of walls, the rectangular shapes of pictures that previously hung proudly could be spied in darker damask once hidden from the punishing rays of sunlight. The missing pictures hailed to an earlier time, before her husband and her father had met, when the duke had commenced selling off ancestral artifacts to sustain his ailing coffers. It was that very act that had led to Lillian being where she now sat, in a room that even smelled stale itself, the result of having been shut up for some time.

The influx of money from Lillian's dowry would soon cure all these ailments. It was the reason Wentworth had married her, after all. His withdrawal from her had made that more than apparent.

"It has been quite a few years since Wentworth Abbey was opened for Christmas," the housekeeper continued. "The former duke and duchess dearly loved to spend the Yuletide here, but that was some time ago, before the tragedy."

Lillian reached for her teacup. "Of course."

Not knowing what else to say, she took a sip. She was familiar with her husband's family history. Mother made certain of it, just as she made certain that Lillian would accept His Grace's proposal. Both his younger brother and parents had perished at sea during a sailing trip. The duke had been abroad at the time. He had returned from the Continent an orphan.

Perhaps that was why he was so aloof and difficult to know.

"Would you care to review the menu for the week, considering that His Grace will be arriving later today?" Mrs. Greaves asked.

Lillian choked on her tea, nearly spitting it ungracefully back into the cup. "Forgive me. I must have misheard you. I thought you said His Grace would be arriving later today."

"You didn't mishear me, Your Grace."

"His Grace, my husband?"

Husband still felt strange on her tongue, a bit like the poisonous berry she once picked at her family's summer house as a child and placed in her mouth because her older brother had dared her to. *Brothers.* Henry was fortunate she forgave him for nearly orchestrating her untimely demise. She had been wise enough to spit it out after she collected her prize, which happened to be a ribbon candy he'd been keeping in his pocket.

She issued a silent prayer that the housekeeper was referring to some other duke. To *any* other duke. Surely she wasn't speaking of the Duke of Wentworth.

Mrs. Greaves's brows snapped together. "Of course, Your Grace. He sent word of his impending arrival a fortnight ago. I assumed the two of you had planned your visit accordingly."

No, they had not.

In fact, the only thing they *had* planned was that they would avoid each other. Indeed, they had been doing so with great success for the last month, and Lillian had no desire for their mutual separation to end.

She forced a smile for the housekeeper's benefit, her mother's years of ceaseless training returning to her. "Oh yes, we did indeed. I had merely failed to realize that His Grace would be joining me here at Wentworth Abbey so soon."

"He is expected within the hour."

Within the hour?

A fluttering started in her belly. A ridiculous, irritating sensation she never seemed able to control, regardless of how much she disliked the man who was apparently determined to ruin her Christmas solitude.

The man who had kissed her with such overwhelming passion, making her burn for him, only to revert to his cool, reserved state once again. As if it had never happened. Seven months ago, and Lillian still could not forget the way he had set her aflame.

She gritted her teeth now. "Perhaps you might wish to review the menu with His Grace instead, then."

"He asked me to defer to you."

Lillian clenched her jaw. "Naturally. Well, Mrs. Greaves, I have every confidence in your ability to plan a menu that will be more than suitable for the occasion. Have Cook prepare His Grace's favorite dishes."

And I will do my best to refrain from dumping any of them on his head.

She didn't dare say that aloud, however.

"I will do so, but are there any dishes that Your Grace would like to request?" Mrs. Greaves asked with her omnipresent polite patience.

"None that I can presently think of," Lillian reassured her grimly.

Her mind whirled, plotting escape. If Wentworth intended to spend Christmas at Wentworth Abbey, she would simply go elsewhere. Perhaps back to London. There must have been some sort of miscommunication between them. Why else would he come to Hertfordshire when she wrote him with her intention to spend the Christmas season there?

Likely, he had failed to read the missive she sent him.

A sudden commotion rose from beyond the sad little

sitting room, and her body seized, like a watch spring tightly coiled.

Mrs. Greaves brightened. "That would be His Grace now!"

Lillian couldn't manage to summon even a hint of the housekeeper's enthusiasm. What was Wentworth doing here?

"How wonderful," she drawled without any accompanying emotion, when all she truly meant was *how terrible*.

It was going to be a long Christmas.

❄

It had been a bloody long train ride to Wentworth Abbey, and all Alaric wanted to do was crawl into the nearest bed and sleep.

But when one had been born the eleventh Duke of Wentworth, that simply wasn't done. Instead, one affected a congenial persona and greeted his domestics, who were all pleased with him for at last opening up the moldering country estate he had largely abandoned.

Because his wife had wished it.

Ah, yes. Lillian Amelia, now the eleventh Duchess of Wentworth. The woman he had married a month ago in an opulent spectacle of New York City wealth. The woman who hadn't wanted to marry him. The woman who was in love with someone else. Some nameless, faceless suitor. The knowledge that her heart was reserved for another still stung.

There she was now, hovering at the periphery of the servants with Mrs. Greaves. Her blonde tresses were plaited into Grecian braids and confined in a knot at her crown. Her summer-berry lips were pinched with slight distaste, almost as if she'd taken a bite of something spoiled. Her pale-blue eyes were unreadable as they met his over the sea of smiling maids and footmen.

His wife must have been busy procuring additional help. Just as well. As the daughter of a hideously wealthy American businessman, Lillian was accustomed to a phalanx of servants catering to her every whim. Whilst he, on the other hand, had spent much of his life on the edge of penury. The Dukes of Wentworth were once proud and rich as Croesus, but that was centuries ago, before his profligate predecessors had wasted their funds on gambling, drink, and wenches, though not always in that order. Before the crops had failed. Before the estates had begun to tumble headlong into ruin.

The servants parted neatly, coaxed by Mrs. Greaves. Alaric strolled up the avenue they had created in the great hall, stopping before his wife and offering her the most gentlemanly bow he could muster. She curtseyed in response. They were the politest two souls ever to have graced the marble floor of this grand estate.

Because they were strangers. The fault for that lay with both of them. But he was here to rectify it now. He hadn't married her because he had fallen in love with her. That had come frighteningly quickly, somewhere between their first meeting and the day he had taken her into his arms in a New York City mansion, only to have his feelings summarily dashed like a ship on rocky shoals. He had married her because he needed her dowry to save his estates and because he needed an heir. Alaric had already set to work on the first objective over the last month, and now it was time to see to the second.

"Madam," he greeted her.

Lillian gave him her hand as regally as a queen, never mind a duchess. He grasped her fingers lightly with his, pressing a chaste kiss to her bare skin. The faint scent of jasmine danced along his senses, pleasant and familiar, taking him back to the kisses they had shared upon the signing of their betrothal contract, before everything had gone so hopelessly awry.

"Your Grace," she responded, jerking her hand from his hold.

A slight pink tinge had risen on her elegant cheekbones. Her countenance gave no indication of what she might be thinking beneath the lovely mask. The former Miss Lillian Penrose was a celebrated beauty. The newspapers had been filled with flowery descriptions of her glorious face and figure. She hailed from the cream of New York high society, and aside from the size of her dowry and the fact she loved someone else, Alaric knew scarcely anything about her.

"You are well, I trust?" he asked her politely.

Her letters to him had all been succinct and impersonal. She looked healthy, if not happy. Dimly, he recalled her mother relaying a concern that their *curious English weather*, as she had called it, would not be suited to her darling daughter's fragile constitution. The worry hadn't been sufficient to prevent Mrs. Augustus Penrose from marrying her daughter off to the first duke she'd found, however.

"I am quite well, thank you, Your Grace," his wife said, unsmiling.

She issued this reassurance in a voice she may have also used to say something like *I adore being bitten by spiders and swimming with leeches, Your Grace. Have I mentioned I would dearly love to be eaten by a bear?*

"I am relieved to hear it," he offered, feeling equally stiff and formal.

She said nothing in return, simply staring at him as an awkward silence unfolded. Not for the first time, he wondered if the woman he had married cared for him at all. Perhaps the passion she had shown him had been nothing more than an act. He had told himself, again and again, that it must have been.

Alaric turned to the faithful housekeeper who had been with his family for over twenty years, genuinely pleased to see her. "Mrs. Greaves. I must thank you for the warm welcome from the domestics."

"It is our pleasure. We are so very pleased that you and Her Grace are spending Christmas at Wentworth Abbey," Mrs. Greaves replied, her countenance the opposite of his wife's.

"As am I," he lied, grinning through a clenched jaw for the sake of his housekeeper and the rest of the servants.

Alaric ventured another glance in his wife's direction to find her staring at him. Their gazes clashed, and awareness jolted through him. Lillian was incredibly attractive, though almost a bit too perfect. Her silk Worth gown was no doubt the height of Parisian fashion, a pale green that hugged her shape, ornamented with jet beads and black lace. Briefly, he wondered if she still yearned for her lover.

Their wedding had been the talk of New York City society. During his miserable tenure abroad, he had read the papers so he could learn about their impending nuptials. He'd had no hand in the planning of it. He had merely been told when to arrive and where to stand. It had suited Alaric well enough. Had there been nary a single flower decking the church pews instead of thousands, he wouldn't have given a damn. His purpose had been to wed her.

And that, he had done, even if he had still yet to bed her.

"Your valises will be sent to your chamber, Your Grace," Mrs. Greaves informed him brightly. "The ducal apartments have been aired out and cleaned in anticipation of your arrival."

"Thank you, Mrs. Greaves. Perhaps you would see a tray of tea brought to the gold salon for Her Grace and myself?"

He didn't miss his wife's eyes widening at his suggestion. Likely, she'd hoped he wouldn't require any of her time or attention. But they had been married for...*damn it all*. An entire month.

And it was more than past time he did his duty in consummating their marriage.

Even if he didn't want to.

CHAPTER 2

NEW YORK CITY EIGHT MONTHS EARLIER

"The Duke of Wentworth is here to see you, my darling girl."

Lillian started at the voice of her mother, the action causing her paint brush to send a line of emerald across the roses she had just perfected.

"Drat," she muttered, heaving a sigh.

Mother sailed across the room to where Lillian had set up her paint set and easel, by the window with the most advantageous light. "Lillian, what in heaven's name are you wearing?"

She glanced down at her gown, a comfortable day silk that was several years old. "I'm wearing one of my painting gowns. Why should it matter?"

"Because His Grace is waiting for you in the front drawing room."

The front drawing room was where Mother received guests who were of the utmost importance, as opposed to the other two drawing rooms Father had made certain his architect had also built at her direction. Belatedly, it occurred to her why her mother was in such a state. The duke she had been determined that Lillian must wed, the impoverished aristocrat who had been lured to New York City by the promise of Father's boundless wealth, was here.

In this very house. Bother. It would seem that the future she had been doing her utmost to avoid and ignore was hurtling toward her, faster than she could have fathomed even yesterday.

She began repainting the roses. "Why is he here? I thought he was in England."

Mother reached her. "Lillian, you have paint on your cheek."

She glanced up to see her mother frowning ferociously at her.

"I do?"

"You do," Mother snapped. "You look a fright. What are you doing, painting at a time like this? Put that brush down. Oh, what a disaster this is. His Grace will take one look at you and refuse the match, I know it."

"I shouldn't mind if he did."

"Lillian Penrose, how dare you utter such nonsense?"

Lillian sighed. "Because I don't want to be sold like a cow at market."

"*Sold like a cow*," Mother gasped, trembling with affront. "I won't hear anything of the sort. You are not being sold. You are being *considered* by His Grace. I need not tell you that it is a vast and enviable honor that most young ladies would give all their finest gowns and jewels to have. You will be the talk of Society."

Just as Mother so fervently wished.

Never mind what Lillian wanted.

She dipped her paintbrush into her water jar, rinsing it. "Yes, they will all be whispering behind their fans about how terrible it is that my father is bartering me for a title."

"No one is bartering you. Not another word, do you hear

me? Now put down that brush and go and change into something more suitable to receive him." Mother was so distraught that she was wringing her hands. "Tell Jacinda that she must try something with your hair. It looks as if a gathering of squirrels has taken up residence in it."

Now it was Lillian's turn to frown. "I prefer to wear my hair this way."

"The duke will take one look at you and run straight to the nearest ship to sail back to England."

"I would dearly love it if he would," she drawled.

Mother regarded her with stern disapproval, her mouth thinned to a small, tight line. "You will go to your room and change out of this gown, and you will have Jacinda tidy your hair into a presentable style, and you will come to the front drawing room wearing a smile."

"Or?"

"Or your painting lessons with Monsieur Dupont will come to an end," Mother snapped.

Lillian froze. Did her mother know that she had been harboring a certain fondness for her handsome, French painting instructor? Surely Lillian hadn't made her inconvenient, burgeoning feelings known. Had she? He was so talented, and he thought Lillian's work was impressive.

"Monsieur Dupont is a master, and I am fortunate to work under his tutelage," she protested, keeping her expression carefully neutral. "He has said I possess an innate talent that he's never seen before in one of his students."

It was the wrong thing to say, because Mother's eyes narrowed and her nostrils flared, telling signs she was gravely displeased. "Has he been untoward with you?"

"Of course not." Indeed, Lillian didn't even think Monsieur Dupont was aware of her interest in him. Certainly, if he were, he had never shown it. He had been a consummate gentleman.

"Of course not," Mother repeated in a tone that suggested she didn't believe Lillian's denial for a moment. "Lillian, go upstairs now and see that you return looking like a young lady who is worthy of becoming a duchess."

"What if I don't want to be one?"

Mother gave her a small, pained smile. "You will in time, my dear. Now go."

"If I don't?"

"If you don't, then Monsieur Dupont will not merely find himself removed from his post as your painting instructor. He will also find that not one door in this entire city will open to him. Ever again."

Lillian sucked in a breath, shocked at the vehemence in her mother's voice as much as the threat. "But that would ruin him."

Mother smiled grimly. "Precisely. If you don't wish for that to happen, then you will do as I say and go."

Lillian knew better than to argue with her mother. If Mother had decided Monsieur Dupont was finished in New York City, he would be, and Lillian wouldn't be able to do anything to stop his professional demise from happening. One word from Mrs. Augustus Penrose was all such a damning feat would require.

Lillian left the salon at once for the sanctity of her bedroom, where she dressed in one of her most severe gowns. A mourning gown of dour black, buttoned to the throat. She instructed Jacinda to pull her hair tightly into a chignon, using none of the artifice she ordinarily employed when she helped Lillian to dress for balls and other society events. The result staring back at her in the looking glass would hopefully be sufficient to send the duke on his way.

❄

THE FIRST TIME ALARIC ROTHWELL, Duke of Wentworth, set eyes upon the woman he hoped to wed, she looked rather like a woman about to attend a funeral instead of a lady receiving a suitor. Still, there was no mistaking the breathtaking beauty she had been rumored to possess. In this instance, gossip was not wrong.

Her eyes were a faded Prussian blue, light and striking, framed by luxurious golden lashes. Despite the unbecoming manner in which her hair had been scraped to her perfectly shaped head, her blonde tresses complemented her creamy skin and summer-berry lips. She was shorter than he had anticipated when compared to his height, but then, Alaric was accustomed to towering over most members of his acquaintance.

Her waist had been cinched to a waspish hourglass, and she moved with an ethereal grace that suggested she hailed from an otherworldly realm. She possessed a retroussé nose, a dimpled chin, and high cheekbones. The overall effect was a face he had no doubt any artist would love to paint.

At least his future duchess was pleasant to look upon. Presently, it didn't appear as if the same pleasantness could be ascribed to her personality as well. She was grim and aloof, unsmiling.

Alaric bowed. "Mrs. Penrose, Miss Penrose."

Lillian Penrose's mother presided over their introduction rather like a procuress at a brothel. Albeit a procuress who was swathed in the finest silk and Parisian fashion whilst dripping in diamonds. So many diamonds that as she moved, the lamplight caught in their facets, making Alaric think wryly that it was a miracle all those priceless stones didn't blind him.

"Your Grace," Mrs. Penrose returned, bowing her head in deference as if Alaric were a king gracing their massive New York City manse.

In truth, he was but an impoverished duke who had been lured to these shores by the promise of salvation. He had been in the process of selling off all remaining paintings of value, along with the immense Wentworth library, when Mr. Augustus Penrose, hideously wealthy real estate magnate and railroad baron, had made Alaric an offer he hadn't been able to refuse. Penrose was a collector of fine art and antiquities, but he was also the father of a marriageable-age daughter.

"What if you were able to keep these familial treasures where they belong?" Penrose had asked slyly.

"Impossible," Alaric had said, having struggled for the last few years to avoid selling off anything he could to keep the estates running.

"Visit me in New York City," Penrose had urged. *"I suspect you might enjoy meeting my daughter, Miss Lillian Amelia Penrose."*

And here Alaric was, meeting the celebrated beauty who was reported on quite thoroughly in the city gossip rags.

"How lovely it is to make your acquaintances," he said formally.

Miss Penrose was looking at a point over his shoulder rather than directly at him. Wryly, Alaric wondered if she feared he was a Gorgon who would turn her to stone if she but met his gaze.

"We are honored by your call, Your Grace," Mrs. Penrose said.

Miss Penrose remained silent, her full lips pinched as if she were holding in a humorless laugh. Alaric was not accustomed to being ignored by the fairer sex. The sensation was novel. He didn't think he liked it very much.

Particularly not regarding the woman he intended to wed.

"Lillian," Mrs. Penrose prodded her daughter in a low voice, teeth gritted as she kept her welcoming hostess's smile pinned tightly to her lips.

Miss Penrose blinked, at last turning the full force of her gaze upon him. "We are honored, Your Grace."

There was nothing impolite in her tone or carriage. He could find no fault in her manner, in her dress. And yet, he could not shake the feeling that Miss Penrose didn't wish to be here.

"Tea should be arriving shortly," Mrs. Penrose offered brightly. "Our housekeeper has a matter of some import that requires my attention. I'll be gone but a few moments. If you will excuse me?"

Alaric inclined his head. "Of course, madam."

Mrs. Penrose swept from the room with the regal authority of a queen, and well she may have been because if what Alaric had read was true, the woman ruled over the upper echelons of New York City society as if she were indeed a sovereign matriarch.

It was also blatantly apparent she wished to give her daughter and Alaric some time alone in each other's company.

When Mrs. Penrose was gone, Alaric offered Miss Penrose his arm. "Perhaps we might sit and get better acquainted."

She eyed his arm as if it were a befouled shoe. "Is there a reason for us to become better acquainted?"

"Your father may have mentioned that I am in need of a wife."

"In need of a fortune, you mean."

That was appallingly direct of her. He felt the sting of her words like an arrow winging into his flesh, hitting their mark.

He inclined his head. "In need of restoring my estates to their former glory, yes."

"Are there not other heiresses in this town whom you might choose for the dubious honor of funding your estates with their dowries instead?" she asked with disinterest.

Alaric nearly choked. "Undoubtedly, there are, Miss Penrose. However, your father expressed a desire for the two of us to become better acquainted."

It was the most politic way of saying that the cunning Mr. Augustus Penrose had essentially bribed Alaric into this visit. He had offered Alaric a loan to restore the roof at Wentworth Abbey. In desperation, Alaric had accepted the funds, understanding full well that they came with a price all their own.

"Keep the paintings and the library here for now," Penrose had said, smiling faintly. "Come to New York City. If all goes well, they may remain here, and the loan will be forgiven."

Alaric needed a wife. A wealthy wife. He also required heirs to carry on the family line. In the end, he hadn't had a choice at all.

"How well do you know my father?" Miss Penrose wanted to know, her tone wary.

"We met when he was in England attending to business matters. He came to my estate with the intent of purchasing some antiquities I was selling."

That much was the truth.

"Perhaps not well enough to know that my father is adept at getting what he wants in all matters, even if it comes to marrying off his daughter," Miss Penrose said archly.

"I trust that his daughter doesn't wish to be married off, given your response," Alaric drawled, amused by her daring.

No English miss of his acquaintance would have been so forthright. He found Miss Penrose's candor oddly endearing.

She raked him with an assessing stare that was equally bold. "I suppose that remains to be seen, Your Grace."

Mrs. Penrose bustled back into the drawing room, accompanied by servants bearing a tea tray. She beamed when she took in Alaric and her daughter in proximity, clearly joining her husband in her desire to see Miss Penrose married to a duke.

"Let's enjoy tea, shall we?" she asked.

"Tea would be lovely," Alaric told his hostess, even though the last thing he wanted to do at present was to suffer through a cup of tepid tea with a matchmaking mama and the daughter who clearly didn't want to marry him.

It was, he thought, a rather inauspicious beginning.

And yet, there was some indefinable quality about Miss Lillian Penrose that he found oddly refreshing and strangely irresistible. He was inexplicably drawn to her, moved by her audacious air and pragmatism.

Perhaps there would be hope for the two of them yet.

CHAPTER 3

ENGLAND 1889

*L*illian prepared the tea while the duke watched in flinty silence. His dark eyes followed her every movement. Was he judging her? Finding her unaccomplished? Woefully lacking in the genteel arts required of a duchess? Or perhaps waiting for her to make a mistake?

She didn't know.

His expression betrayed nothing of his feelings. He was impervious as stone, his jaw hewn of granite. If she could describe the Duke of Wentworth in a word, it would be *brooding*. His thick, dark hair was neatly cropped. His jaw bore a shadow of whiskers, as if he had last shaved yesterday or perhaps even the day before. His lips were almost too large, though well-formed.

She had kissed them.

Once.

It had been so many months ago now that those soul-altering kisses might never have happened.

But they had, and she hadn't been able to control her body's reaction to that wild moment when their mouths had met. She had gasped, shocked at the way heat flooded over her, by how pleasant his lips had felt, warm and firm on hers. And then too quickly, he had stepped away, the betrothal had been sealed, and she had never again glimpsed the passionate man who had stolen her breath so thoroughly. The ardent lover had been replaced by a removed stranger, one who hardly smiled and who never touched anything more than her hand. One who had married her only to leave her.

Lillian's hand trembled slightly as she passed her husband his tea.

His fingers, now bereft of gloves, grazed hers as he accepted. "Thank you."

His voice was deep and pleasant, and although she tried to remain unaffected by his aristocratic accent, it was an almost impossible feat. He could have uttered something as crass as *cow dung*, and it would still somehow have sounded sensual. How could he remain so unmoved when his mere presence made the world feel as if it had tipped.

She forced a smile that likely more resembled a grimace. "You're welcome, Your Grace."

"Alaric."

She flicked a glance in his direction, poised to pour a cup of tea for herself. "I beg your pardon?"

"It seems unnecessary to insist upon formality," he explained. "We are husband and wife. You may as well call me by my given name, and I shall call you Lillian."

It was the first time he had spoken her name instead of the stiff and proper *Miss Penrose* or *madam*.

Hearing it in his mellifluous baritone felt oddly intimate. She liked it far too much, and she didn't trust herself where Wentworth was concerned.

"I will defer to your preferences in the matter." She poured, distracting herself.

Lillian had no notion why the duke had come to Wentworth Abbey. Nor why he had insisted upon a private tea together. And she certainly didn't understand why, after a month of absence, he had reappeared in her life, requesting that they call each other by their given names.

His presence in her life was an unprecedented sea change. It made her nervous. And foolishly hopeful, even if she had no reason for it.

"Have you no preferences?" he asked.

She glanced up at him. He stared at her in an unnerving way, as if he could somehow see into her. He was incredibly attractive, the man she had been forced to marry. Little wonder he was England's most eligible bachelor. His family name was well-known, the history spanning centuries. But more than that, the Duke of Wentworth—Alaric—was handsome.

Not just handsome.

Despicably handsome. Maddeningly so. He was the sort of handsome that seemed impossible. He possessed the kind of good looks that made matrons and debutantes alike swoon over him in the ballroom. Kittens and puppies probably wept at his feet.

Lillian's cup ran over, jolting her from her thoughts.

Hastily, she jerked her gaze from him.

He was to blame for her lack of grace. He was so lovely to look upon she couldn't even pour a proper cup of tea. She was badly flustered as she reached for a cloth serviette and hastily sopped up the hot liquid.

Why *was* he here?

"I'm sorry," she apologized, feeling as if she had failed her first test as a duchess.

This was the longest they had been in a room together since they'd married.

"Here. Allow me." His hands suddenly took hers, gently moving them away as he carefully blotted the tea.

She hadn't expected him to offer his assistance. Lillian sat stiffly as she watched him make short work of cleaning up the mess she had made.

"There we are," he announced with a smile that showed off his dimples.

Twin, perfect dimples that bracketed his mouth.

She yearned to throw one of the cucumber sandwiches arranged on a tray between them at his head.

She didn't give in to the temptation, however.

Instead, she played the part she had been taught so well—dutiful wife.

"Thank you," Lillian told him politely. "I must confess, I was surprised when I learned you would be joining me here at Wentworth Abbey. Had I known you intended to be in residence, I could have stayed in London."

Her husband took a sip of his tea, and even the way he drank was mesmerizing. She watched the dip of his Adam's apple as he swallowed.

"When you informed me of your plan to pass the Christmas season here, I decided it would be most expedient to join you."

So, he had intended to come here, knowing she had planned to isolate herself in the country. She couldn't begin to imagine why. They had spent nearly the entirety of their marriage apart thus far, aside from the passage across the Atlantic, which Lillian had largely spent in seasick misery.

"And yet, you only saw fit to inform Mrs. Greaves of your plans," she pointed out, unable to keep her irritation to herself.

The housekeeper had known, and she had not. How little he must think of her.

"There wasn't sufficient time, I'm afraid."

Her husband appeared to think nothing was wrong with his actions. Lillian didn't know why she was surprised. He had also thought it perfectly proper to abandon her in London upon their arrival and to flee to Scotland.

They hadn't even had a honeymoon. He had simply gone.

"But there *was* enough time to send a message to your housekeeper," she said.

Mother would have been horrified with her for being so bold. Lillian was to hold her tongue and allow her husband to treat her as he liked. It was his prerogative, and certainly, it was what she had done with Father. But she found her patience growing ever thinner. She had been a dutiful daughter first and then a dutiful duchess, even when she'd had no wish to be one.

He stilled, staring at her intently. "You're displeased."

"I didn't think you would be here."

That was unkind of her to say, even if it was true.

His dark brows drew together. "Where else would I be?"

"I don't know," she bit out, unable to keep the annoyance from her voice. "Where else have you been this last month?"

"Only at Fernross Castle, of course. Scotland was where I was needed, thanks to your father. I don't suppose he might have been more judicious in his timing, but perhaps it worked out for the best."

Lillian remembered their conversation a month prior, during which the world had still been rocking like a ship beneath her. She had been dreadfully out of sorts for an entire week after their arrival in England, waking each night to a strange bed, her surroundings cloaked in darkness, the earth seemingly shifting as if she were yet upon the sea.

She recalled lying in bed, her lady's maid bringing her tea she hadn't the stomach to even drink. Her husband had come to her, aloof as ever, politely inquiring over her welfare.

She'd reassured him that she was well, merely still recovering from the ordeal of transatlantic travel. He'd expressed a need to do something her father required of him—perhaps a meeting with the architect, though her memory remained as foggy as London. Their honeymoon would have to wait, he had said. There were far too many tasks awaiting him.

She had agreed.

But it had been his parting words that had stayed with her, the ones that had felt a bit like a dagger sinking into her tender heart at the time.

Some time apart will be just the thing, my dear. We both need time, I suspect, to adjust to this marriage.

The time he'd required had been a day, then a week, until it had finally become an entire month. Lillian had begun to think his defection would last forever. The duke's somewhat cavalier treatment of her wasn't supposed to have hurt, and yet, her coat of armor hadn't been capable of withstanding such blows.

"My father is only judicious in matters of business, I'm afraid," she said. "Likely, he was more concerned with the visit he and Mother intend to pay us. She is overjoyed at the prospect of her daughter living in a medieval palace that once housed kings and queens."

"Yes, I can see that she would be. Your mother is quite unashamed of her social aspirations. No doubt she plans to rub the noses of friend and foe alike back in New York after her visit."

Lillian smiled faintly. "I'm sure it has already begun. She has been writing to me, overjoyed at the prospect. I do hope that there will be a room large enough for the fifty trunks she plans to bring with her."

"I'm afraid there is only sufficient room for thirty or so."

Lillian stared at him, uncertain if he was making a joke or serious.

But then he smiled faintly, and his dimples reappeared, and she tried not to notice. "I hope you were overestimating the number of cases Mrs. Penrose brings with her on her trips."

"I was," she said, keeping her expression carefully blank. "By perhaps one or two."

He chuckled and they settled into an almost companionable silence. Lillian thought again about the month he had been gone. Each week that had added upon the last had chipped away at her patience, until it had grown brittle and thin.

"Why did my father think it necessary for you to travel to Scotland? I don't recall you mentioning it before you left."

Her husband sipped his tea, frowning. "He wanted me to confer with the architect directly. There is a great deal of history at Fernross Castle, and we often differed over what we would change and what we would restore. Your father requested that I remain there for the first few weeks, to at least make certain all would progress well."

Of course, her father had his hands in this. She might have known. After all, he and Wentworth had arranged the marriage settlement and betrothal without Lillian's participation. Some of the hurt that had been festering within her at her husband's month-long absence faded. But still, it had been Wentworth's choice to remain in Scotland for as long as he had. To leave her in London.

She raised a brow. "My father required you to remain there for a whole month?"

"There is much to be done at the castle in preparation for the visit from your parents next summer. Besides that, it had been some time since I had ventured to Scotland. I met with my steward, toured the estate, spoke with tenants."

Meanwhile, she had spent the duration of her time in England alone, muddling her way through her new duties, homes, and servants while trying to live up to the expectations of her mother. It was difficult not to be insulted that he had chosen to travel to Scotland alone.

"I don't understand," she said, summoning what remained of her patience. "It sounds as if you had a great deal to occupy you at Fernross Castle. Why did you journey here to Wentworth Abbey?"

"Because you're here."

His dark eyes burned into Lillian, holding her captive.

There was somehow an underlying intimacy in his voice, in his stare. It sent something sharp and warm through her, a sensation she'd experienced before, when he had kissed her. One that she had ruthlessly tamped down and banished in an effort to guard her ever-fragile heart.

One that had been easy to forget in his absence and was proving difficult to ignore, given his current proximity.

She took a deep breath and dismissed all unwanted feelings. "Forgive me if I fail to see what my presence here has to do with anything."

"You're my wife."

"I am aware." Painfully so.

He smiled, and his dimples emerged. "It's time for me to attend to my husbandly duties."

All the air fled her lungs. The teacup and saucer fell from her suddenly numb fingers. They clattered together on the faded Axminster, chips of porcelain flying as her tea darkened the patterned wool.

❋

Blast.

This reunion with his wife wasn't unfolding as he had hoped it would. This was the second time she'd spilled tea in one quarter hour.

But could he blame Lillian? He had all but announced his intentions to shag her over tea.

"I'll ring for a maid," Alaric announced, feeling foolish as he abandoned his cup and crossed the room to the bellpull.

"Forgive me," she murmured, leaping from her seat as if it suddenly caught flame. "I don't know why I'm being so clumsy."

"It would seem I have that effect on you," he offered, trying to make a jest of the miserable situation in which they had found themselves.

Over the course of their betrothal and marriage, Lillian had been guarded, aloof, and painfully polite to him. And although he had learned the reason when he'd unintentionally discovered the letter from her erstwhile suitor, Alaric hadn't realized that the notion of bedding him would be so distressing to her. He had hoped that swallowing his pride and giving her time and distance would help to ease her into her new role as his duchess.

It would seem he had been wrong.

"Surely you agree that we must spend time together as husband and wife," he added in a softer tone when she said nothing, simply stared at him as if he had sprouted into a mysterious creature before her. "I had no wish to spend Christmastide in a draughty castle with an architect when I can spend it here with my wife."

That was not precisely the truth.

He hadn't come here to hang mistletoe and gather presents around a tree. He hardly expected domestic bliss and undying devotion from Lillian, given that she harbored feelings for someone else.

He had come to Wentworth Abbey because he was obligated to do so. Because he had been a husband for an entire month, and he had yet to consummate their marriage. And if he didn't consummate the marriage, he couldn't have an heir.

And if he couldn't have an heir, he would have failed past and future Dukes of Wentworth.

The line would die with him.

He couldn't allow that. Familial duty flowed in his blood.

"Of course," his wife said faintly, wearing an icy mask of indifference.

He wondered what, if anything, moved her. Would she lie silently and rigid as a board in bed? God, he hoped not. There had been the fiery promise of the kisses they had shared at their betrothal. But the promise had faded like an autumn bloom after first frost when he'd discovered that bloody letter.

A chambermaid entered the room, efficiently taking care of the spill and sweeping up the shards of porcelain before quietly excusing herself.

Alaric waited until she had gone and was firmly out of listening range, the silence between Lillian and himself hanging heavier than a pall at a funeral.

The door closed quietly.

His wife stared at the tea tray. What was she thinking? There was surely a more eloquent, perhaps even charming means of announcing his intentions. But then, she also had to realize that theirs was not a marriage in name only. She must have known he would require an heir at some point, and that there was only one means of securing his line.

Ensuring he had heirs was one of the two practical reasons he had married her. The third, wildly impractical reason had been that he had fallen in love with her, never mind that his feelings were not returned. But that was a secret he intended to take to his grave.

He cleared his throat. "It wasn't my intention to distress you, Lillian."

She summoned a smile he suspected was for his benefit.

"You haven't distressed me, Your Grace. I'm more than aware of my duties."

He didn't prefer her to think of him bedding her as a *duty*. But there they were, joined by their mutual familial obligations. He wished he could unlove her, but unfortunately, there was no civility in emotions. They were like wild, rampaging beasts, doing as they willed without regard for repercussions.

"Excellent," he managed tightly in response. "You may speak with Mrs. Greaves concerning the preparations for Christmas. Decorate as you see fit."

"Did your mother decorate?" she asked.

The question, though an innocent one, spurred a stab of lingering anguish deep within him. "She did, yes."

Alaric's mother had been a wonderful woman. She had also been flighty, with a propensity for spending money as if it were water. After his parents' deaths, he had learned that much of the recent ducal debts had been caused by her affinity for French gowns and jewels. Those long-ago Christmastides with his mother had been laden with gifts, festooned with garlands, and decked with mistletoe. There had been carols and singing, sweets and tales by the fireside.

He had never particularly cared for the season after he had lost the entirety of his family to the tragedy.

"I am sorry," Lillian said now, pity flashing over her expressive face. "It wasn't my intention to dredge up painful memories."

"We will forge new memories here at Wentworth Abbey," he said stiffly. "Together."

"Of course," she repeated.

And then they sat in silence once more, as politely miserable as two married strangers could be, his imbecilic love for her glinting as brightly as all the stars in the night sky combined.

CHAPTER 4

NEW YORK CITY SEVEN MONTHS EARLIER

One month of a courtship, and Lillian didn't feel as if she knew the Duke of Wentworth any better than she had when they had first met in the front drawing room.

But that didn't matter.

Because she was now, by the strokes of two pens, engaged to marry him. It would be the society wedding of the year. Mother was already gleefully planning.

The duke stood by the desk where they had so recently signed their lives away, whilst Lillian was sentinel at the window, watching carriages rumble by in the streets below. The day was a rainy one, the sky grim and gray, and thoroughly suited to her mood.

"You have paid me an incredible honor, Miss Penrose," Wentworth said to her, his tone formal as always.

His voice stole her from her rumination, making her turn to him. He was so perfectly well-mannered, whether they were in a crowd of others or alone. Presently, it was just the two of them in the elegant confines of the salon that had doubled as her painting room on so many occasions. Her mahogany box of watercolors and brushes would be crated up and sent to England soon in preparation of her new life as the Duchess of Wentworth.

Everything would change.

"Tell me, Your Grace," she said, studying him curiously. "Are you happy?"

Undoubtedly, it was not the sort of question a newly engaged woman often asked the man who would be her husband. But theirs had not been an ordinary courtship, and she knew that their marriage wouldn't be any different.

They were two strangers, joining their lives together.

He moved toward her, hands clasped behind his back, handsome and tall. She couldn't find fault with the duke's appearance, even if she did with their circumstances. His dark hair was swept back from his high forehead, and he possessed a brooding air that lured women to him as much as his lofty title did. She had watched, at every ball they had both attended, as debutantes and widows alike had fawned over him. His shoulders were broad, his figure lean, his jaw strong.

"I am well pleased, Miss Penrose," he said.

An interesting response indeed, and telling, too.

"But not happy," she pressed.

Silence fell between them, interrupted only by the drumming of the rain on the windowpane at her side.

"Are *you* happy?" he countered, instead of answering her question.

She wished she knew the meaning of his deflection. Aside from a handful of polite conversations, they hadn't spoken directly to each other very often.

Lillian thought of Monsieur Dupont, to whom she had written after Mother had abruptly canceled all future painting lessons. He had responded, and his letter had soundly crushed any hopes she may have still harbored that he had cared for her. Even worse, Mother had shown her proof that Monsieur Dupont had accepted a handsome sum to leave the city and never speak with her again. It had been a foolish fancy, the way she'd felt for the handsome painting instructor. She had always known it, but her pride was quite battered just the same.

And her heart was ragged and worn, incredibly wary of the duke before her.

Willing, perhaps, to open to him.

One day.

"No," she answered honestly. "I am not happy. It was not my wish to marry a man who lives an ocean away from everything I have known, nor to make my life there."

He stopped at her side, his dark-brown eyes with their sparkling amber depths intent upon hers. "You won't be alone in England. You shall have me."

Would she have him, though? Lillian was not naïve. More than one marriage of convenience had led to a husband taking a mistress or a wife taking a lover. She wondered then if there was anyone Wentworth cared for at home. Did he already have a mistress? Was there another woman in whom he'd had an interest before her father had come along, luring him with the promises that only the Penrose fortune could offer?

"I scarcely know you," she pointed out to the duke instead of airing any of her tumultuous concerns.

"You will know me better in time."

She swallowed hard against a rise of emotion. "This is not the manner of marriage I wanted or imagined I would have."

It wasn't as if Mother hadn't prepared her for it from birth. Lillian had been raised to know her place in the world and to understand what was expected of her. Mother's objective in life was to see to it that she remained the queen on the throne of high society.

"Nor is it the manner of union I would have chosen for

myself," Wentworth conceded, surprising her. "But sometimes life leads us on a path we couldn't have comprehended, even if we cannot fathom the reasons. I find myself looking forward to our union. I hope that you will find every happiness in being my wife." He paused, reaching for her hand and taking it in his. "Have you changed your mind?"

She shook her head. "No, of course not. I haven't."

There was no one else for her. And she was nothing if not a dutiful daughter. She had an obligation to her parents, and she wanted to make them proud.

The duke brought her hand to his lips, kissing her knuckles.

Sparks of awareness jolted up her arm, making her fingers tense on his involuntarily.

"We have the rest of our lives to grow to know each other," he said softly.

And yet, although he held her hand, he was still being polite. Almost insufferably so. Unlike other suitors she'd had in the past, the Duke of Wentworth had never even kissed her. Had not attempted it.

Was it because he didn't find her attractive?

She suddenly wanted to know what it would feel like to know him in a different way. He had been the proper, impeccable suitor this last month. She wanted to shake him from his mask of cool indifference. Lillian wanted…

Oh, she didn't even know what she wanted. Inside, she was a mess of confusion. Yearning and trepidation and curiosity were colliding.

"Do you think we will suit?" she asked, giving voice to the questions brewing within her.

"I hope that we shall."

"Perhaps we should test it now, before it's too late."

His eyebrows rose. "What are you suggesting?"

"That you should kiss me," she blurted.

Her face instantly went hot. What was she thinking, to be so daring? What if he thought her appallingly brazen for proposing something so forward?

"You want me to kiss you," he repeated, his voice low and silken.

A rush went over her, unlike anything she'd ever felt before. The duke's expression shifted, growing more intent.

"Yes." The word left her in a whisper.

"That's an excellent idea." His head dipped toward hers.

"I-it is?" she stammered.

"It is." Another inch and his lips settled on hers.

His mouth was warm. Hot, really. She gasped at the sensation, the sheer rightness and thrill, and he kissed her in truth then. His lips moved over hers with expert precision, as if he had already kissed her a hundred times before. As if he had been born to kiss her and she had equally been born for this moment, when this man she scarcely knew angled his mouth over hers and sipped from her lips as if she were the sweetest dessert he had ever tasted.

As if she were something invaluable. Something to be worshiped. As if each kiss were a revelation. No one had ever kissed her like this. She would forever be transformed, and she knew it. There would be the time before she had known his lips on hers, and then there would be the time after.

He was still holding her hand. Lillian realized her fingers gripped his far too tightly. She let go and grasped his shoulders. They were strong and broad beneath her fingertips, wonderfully masculine. He was tall, so tall, and yet they fit together perfectly. As if she belonged in his arms, tucked into his chest. A frisson of something thrilling and new—dangerous, even—went down her spine.

She hadn't felt this way with anyone else.

His hands settled on her waist, and he deepened the kiss, his mouth angled over hers, his tongue gliding along the seam of her lips. She let him in. Welcomed him, even, and knew the luxurious slide of his tongue against hers, the taste of him, sweet like the tea they had shared before the contract, with a hint of berry tart.

Lillian's lips sought his, coaxing, teasing, tasting. She kissed him as if she were starved for him. As if the world would end if their lips parted. And in that moment, it felt as if the world she'd known had indeed upended, nothing to save her but the man holding her in his arms.

The man she was going to marry.

❄

She tasted sweet.

Alaric kissed Miss Penrose, unable to get enough of her. He was a starving man and she was the feast laid before him.

He would die if he didn't have more.

And so he kissed her and kissed her.

Backed her against the desk, intent upon he knew not what. Ravishing her upon the betrothal agreement? Hardly. But she was intoxicating, and he didn't want to stop. Didn't ever want to remove his mouth from hers.

It had required every bit of control he possessed to keep from kissing her this last month. To watch her from afar, falling a bit more under her spell with each passing day until he had gazed upon her across a crowded ballroom one evening and the truth had revealed itself to him in glaring, startling honesty.

He had fallen in love with Miss Lillian Amelia Penrose.

He had never expected his feelings to develop for her so swiftly. On the day he'd first met her, he had hoped that in time, they would develop a mutual appreciation for each other. Perhaps even a friendship. Alaric had never believed there would be or could be love. But she was dazzling. A brilliant butterfly in a sea of sparrows. She was intelligent and kind, bold and candid. Sparing with her smiles, making him want to earn them.

He fitted his lips over hers, telling her everything he did not yet dare to say with words. Showing her how utterly enchanting he found her. How much he appreciated every facet that made her who she was. How much he couldn't wait to be her husband. He had been careful with her thus far, being a gentleman, giving her time, but now they were betrothed, and she had *asked* him to kiss her, and—

Dimly, he became aware of muffled thuds.

Alaric jerked his lips from hers, eyes flying to the door. But they hadn't been interrupted by a wily chaperone. Neither Mr. nor Mrs. Penrose hovered at the threshold. He and Miss Penrose had likely been left alone for a good reason.

This one.

Never mind that. He was already so smitten with her that he hardly needed a reason to force him into matrimony.

"Oh." Miss Penrose looked up at him, hand pressed to her kiss-swollen lips. Her pale Prussian-blue eyes were wide as they met his.

He found himself grinning at her, pleased by her reaction to his kisses. She had kissed him back, and quite thoroughly, too. Moreover, the idea had been hers.

"Oh, indeed," he echoed, feeling as shocked as she looked.

Their every interaction thus far had been painfully polite to the point of being awkward. He'd thought her frigid. But there was nothing cold about her fiery, passionate response to his kiss.

"I should…I have to…excuse me, Your Grace," she blurted, her cheeks flushed a becoming shade of pink and her rambling words telltale hints that she was every bit as affected as he was.

There would be time aplenty to investigate the undeniable passion burning between them soon. Alaric took a step in retreat, forcing his rampant ardor to cool and putting some much-needed distance between them before he did something truly foolish, like lift her skirts and pleasure her on a desk in the midst of her parents' mansion where anyone could come upon them at any moment.

"Of course, my dear," he said with what he hoped was a passable attempt at sangfroid.

In truth, he felt as if he were at sixes and sevens. The kisses they had just shared had shaken him deeply.

Miss Penrose looked at him as if she meant to say something more. But in the end, she simply curtseyed and fled from the salon, a streak of champagne and ivory silk trailing in her wake. He watched her go, feeling bemused.

Belatedly, Alaric glanced down and found the source of the sound that had forced him to interrupt their kiss. A small stack of books that had been sitting atop the desk had been swept to the floor. Likely by Lillian's billowing bustle and skirts as he had kissed her senseless.

Alaric bent to retrieve the fallen books. As he placed them back atop the desk in their former home, however, one opened and a letter slid from its place tucked within the pages. Thinking to keep the contents of the epistle private, he hastily picked it up, averting his gaze.

But not averting it before he caught a hint of Miss Penrose's name at the top of the page, clearly written in a masculine scrawl. His stomach knotted. She was receiving correspondence from another man?

It was none of his concern, he told himself. She could write to whomever she wished. Letters didn't mean anything.

But as he hastily tucked the letter back into one of the books, his eye caught on one sentence.

Although I hold you in highest regard, I cannot return your eloquently stated feelings. Given your impending marriage to the duke, it is for the best, dearest Lillian, that we should part...

Alaric stuffed the letter deep into the tome's pages without bothering to read the rest, cold replacing the heat that had suffused him.

Alaric was in love with Miss Lillian Penrose.

But she was in love with another nameless, faceless man.

And in six months' time, she would become Alaric's wife.

CHAPTER 5

ENGLAND 1889

Lillian looked up at the massive fir tree that had been brought into the drawing room by the head gardener and half a dozen men. Its branches were huge, extending in all directions. The scent of pine filled the room.

"What do you think, Mrs. Greaves?" she asked the housekeeper, who was hovering at the periphery of the mayhem.

Branches were scattered about, having needed to be clipped to allow the tree through doorways. The gardener, Mr. Richards, eagerly awaited their approval.

"Quite lovely," Mrs. Greaves praised. "It's been years since we've had such a handsome Christmas tree. I cannot help but think His Grace shall be well pleased also."

Lillian bit her lip to keep from blurting that she didn't particularly care whether Wentworth liked the tree or he didn't. She wasn't decorating the manor house for his delectation. She was doing it for herself, because she was lonely and bored and she was spending her first Christmas in a foreign land with a husband she scarcely knew.

A week had passed since the duke's unexpected arrival,

but despite his initial pronouncement that he had joined Lillian at Wentworth Abbey to *spend time together as husband and wife*, little had changed between them. He hadn't visited her bedroom in the evening. He was as indifferent as ever, much to her frustration.

They spent meals at the opposite ends of a grand, carved mahogany table that had been in his family's possession for over one hundred and fifty years. Following dinner, he excused himself to his study, and she retired to the library, where she had been painting, writing letters, and scouring the shelves for any books that could be of interest.

Apparently, the Dukes of Wentworth past harbored an innate fondness for Latin, philosophy, horse breeding, sheep farming, and agriculture. Hence, her painting and letter writing had won the majority of her time. Lillian's friends, at least, would be well amused to hear of her rustication in the English countryside.

"Thank you, Mr. Richards," she offered to the head gardener. "You and your men have done an excellent job of finding us the perfect Christmas tree."

He beamed. "It was our pleasure, Your Grace."

With a bow, he and his men began filing from the drawing room, collecting pruned branches as they went. Footmen arrived next, each bearing a crate of decorations with which to adorn the tree. According to Mrs. Greaves, they had been kept tucked away in the attic in the hope that a new mistress would one day wish to prepare the household for Christmas again.

The maids set to unpacking under Mrs. Greaves's direction, and Lillian decided to help. Before long, they had the candles hung on the tree, along with an assortment of glass ornaments in varying colors. The footmen worked steadily around them, busier than bees in a hive as they adorned the drawing room with more greenery and a kissing bough bearing mistletoe.

By the time they had completed their endeavors, Lillian's lower back was aching and her feet were sore. She thanked the servants for their efforts and settled on a chair by the hearth, enjoying a moment of solitude after so much bustle, the warmth of the crackling fire enveloping her. She had scarcely been seated for any time at all before she heard footsteps entering the room.

Turning her neck to an almost uncomfortable angle, she discovered her husband striding across the Axminster, his gaze fastened upon the towering tree. Wearing country tweed, leather riding boots, and a crisp white shirt beneath his waistcoat, he looked every bit as effortlessly handsome as he had on the day he'd arrived at Wentworth Abbey.

His dark gaze met hers across the room, searing in its intensity, his face an inscrutable mask. "Lillian." He swept into an elegant bow. "I hope I'm not intruding?"

Actually, he *was* interrupting, much as he had by his unexpected arrival at the estate. This was the most solitude she'd enjoyed all day. But there was a vulnerability in his voice that was ordinarily absent, a hesitance that rendered him suddenly far more human than he ordinarily seemed.

The lofty, impenetrable duke's mask had momentarily fallen, and she intended to seize the opportunity. Lillian recalled what Mrs. Greaves had said about it having been years since there had been a Christmas tree at Wentworth Abbey. And suddenly, she suspected she knew the reason for his lack of customary polish and perfection.

"Of course not," Lillian reassured him, summoning a sunny smile that would have done Mother proud as she rose from her seat. "We just finished decorating. What do you think?"

"It's lovely."

He wasn't looking at the tree or the rest of the greenery embellishing the drawing room, however. His gaze was firmly fastened upon her.

His regard sent a rush through her that was familiar by now, an unwelcome reminder that although her husband didn't appear to be interested in her, and despite her stern inward remonstrations that she should remain unaffected by his looks, she was deeply attracted to him.

Lillian cleared her throat, banishing such unwanted feelings. "Thank you, though I can't claim responsibility for most of it. Mrs. Greaves directed us, and Mr. Richards found the tree. He and his men cut it and brought it here into the drawing room."

Wentworth glanced around the room, as if belatedly taking in all the details. "It is just as I remember from when I was a lad."

That same rawness had entered his deep voice.

Impulsively, she reached for him, placing her hand on his sleeve. "Have I overstepped?"

He covered her hand with his, looking back at her with a small, sad smile. "You've done nothing of the sort. Wentworth Abbey is your home now."

It hadn't felt that way when she had initially arrived. But the more time she spent within these old walls, the more she felt as if it truly could be a place where she belonged. More so now that he was here with her, even if he continued in his polite detachment. Lillian had found a certain sense of accomplishment in putting her small touches on the duchess's chamber and in replenishing the domestics so that the staff was proportionate to the manor house's impressive size.

She hadn't expected to enjoy her new role, even if it was what she had been trained for from the time she had been a young girl, watching her mother fasten diamonds at her throat and ears before being passed off to her nursemaid. Lillian's marriage to an English duke had proven the culmination of all Mother's feverish dreams. Never mind what Lillian had wanted for herself, which she hadn't ever had the privilege of learning. The path for her future had been firmly decided at birth. She was a Penrose, after all.

"It is beginning to feel like home," she acknowledged to her husband, keeping the rest of her thoughts to herself.

"I'm glad," he said softly. "After the tragedy, I could scarcely bear to come here. Every corner of Wentworth Abbey was so alive with their memories. It was a bit like living with ghosts, the constant reminder of what might have been. But having you in residence has changed that."

Her ordinarily closed heart ached for him and what he had lost to the unforgiving sea that day. She and Alaric had never shared much of themselves with each other. Their courtship had been largely transactional, like one of her father's business dealings. The duke had paid ceremonious, obligatory calls upon her. He had been the consummate gentleman, always polite, always above reproach.

Then, he had closeted himself away with Father, and the betrothal had been done. She'd had cause to wonder, in the intervening months, if she had been to blame for the coolness between them. There had been that fleeting moment when they'd been alone, where it had seemed as if Wentworth might want her for something more than her tremendous dowry, when he had brought her desires so stunningly to life.

But then, her hopes had been quite firmly dashed. He had withdrawn during the course of their engagement. Even on their wedding day, he had been polite yet oddly removed.

After their betrothal had been formally announced, there hadn't been sufficient time to get to know each other any better. There had been a whirlwind of preparations for the wedding. Dresses to commission, flowers to choose, a guest list to review. There had been a month-long trip to Paris with Mother. Then the culmination of all their efforts—the wedding itself—followed by their journey to England and the duke's defection to Scotland.

"I am pleased if my presence makes it easier," she managed to say.

"It does." His dark gaze was searching on hers, laden with unspoken emotions and something else.

Something that made her heart beat faster.

The very air between them shifted, growing heavier. Hotter.

"Lillian," he murmured, his head dipping toward hers.

He was going to kiss her again. Finally.

She knew it, and...

She *wanted* him to. She wanted to feel his mouth on hers once more. She wanted to know if the sparks within her were capable of catching flame again. Wanted to believe that he might grow to feel something for her, one day. That perhaps there could be more for them than this courteous chill.

He cupped her cheek with one hand, his warmth burning into her. And then, with agonizing slowness, as if he feared she would run away from him, he angled his head toward hers. Their lips meet. The kiss was gentle. Soft and slow.

His mouth on hers was like a homecoming. All these months since that whirlwind of desire in the salon back in New York, and she was every bit as undone now as she had been then. She opened for him, seeking the hot probe of his tongue, wanting to taste him, to devour him. Needing him in a way she hadn't even realized was possible until this moment.

He released her hand, and Lillian was free to touch him. She settled her hands on his broad shoulders, the rough tweed of his coat beneath her fingertips. His scent engulfed her, spicy and pleasant with a hint of musk. Strange to think they had been married for a whole month and yet this was the closest they had been, both physically and emotionally, since their betrothal.

He placed his other hand on her waist, anchoring her to him. He tasted like bergamot and sugar, likely from his tea, and she couldn't keep herself from sighing and moving nearer until her breasts grazed his chest.

The shock of it sent heat to pool between her thighs. She pressed them together to stave off the sensation, but that only seemed to heighten it. Her breasts felt heavy and full, her nipples suddenly aching where they strained stiffly against her corset. Her body had come to life.

For him.

Her husband.

He lifted his head, ending the kiss, and stared down at her, his expression inscrutable. "I should have done that far sooner."

She licked her lips, tasting him. Wanting more. And all she could do was agree.

"Yes, I think you should have."

"Time aplenty to rectify my error now." He brushed his thumb softly over her cheek, and then his mouth was on hers, stealing her breath again.

They kissed until the sound of servants beyond the drawing room, bustling through the halls, intruded on their idyll. And at last, they broke apart, his expression as guilty as she felt for this unexpected display in the midst of day when any of the domestics might come upon them.

"Thank you," he told her quietly.

Lillian didn't know if he was thanking her for the kisses, the decorations in the drawing room, or both.

"You're welcome, Alaric," she returned, not having the courage to ask.

His smile reached his eyes this time. "Would you care to go riding with me?"

It was the first time he had invited her to do anything with him, aside from dining, since their stilted courtship. The day was chilly, the sky leaden, the branches bereft of leaves beyond the windows. But she didn't care. Warmth suffused her.

"I would like that very much."

"Meet me at the stables in an hour."

She nodded and watched as her husband offered her an elegant bow before taking his leave from the room.

Lillian wasn't certain what just happened between them.

But whatever it was, she did know she wanted more of it.

❄

"This was one of my favorite places at Wentworth Abbey when I was a lad," Alaric told Lillian as they walked together along the banks of the river that flowed through the estate.

They had left their horses secured to a tree so they could venture closer to the water. The December air was crisp and cold and damp, but after the kisses they had shared in the drawing room, he needed the chill to quell some of his ardor.

He could only hope that time and distance had cured her heart. That she no longer ached for another. Her responsiveness to his kisses had sent desire careening through him, like a locomotive off its tracks. Nothing could have prepared him for her reaction, for the softness of her lips, for the sweet sigh she'd given him when his tongue had slid against hers.

Kissing Lillian had been like coming home, bittersweet. The betrayal he'd felt over the fallen letter he'd never been meant to see had melted like ice in the spring. Taking its place, lodged deep in his own heart, was hope, that perennial, persistent beast.

"What a beautiful spot," Lillian said at his side, taking in the winding creek and the centuries-old trees presiding over its banks. "I can see why you liked it so much. Did you climb trees and wade into the water in the summer?"

He found a particularly charming location to stop, near a place in the river where the rocks were all worn smooth and the slowly moving waters ran particularly deep.

"It's where I learned to swim with my brother Harry," he confided, thinking about all the sunlit days his younger brother and he had swum and fished and climbed trees.

Their boyhood years had been charmed, which had only made losing his beloved brother that much more difficult. They had been inseparable. The best of friends. And then in the span of a few minutes on the open sea, all that had been taken away so that nothing but the memories remained.

"The two of you were close?" Lillian asked gently.

"We were never in competition, as some siblings are," he told her, staring into the muddy river waters and remembering the sound of Harry's laughter. "He was my champion, and I was his. We did everything we could together."

"You must miss him very much."

"I do." His throat was thick, and he jerked his gaze from the water, settling it upon his wife instead. "And my parents as well."

"Will you tell me about them?"

Speaking about his family was still difficult. For years, his grief had been an albatross he carried around his neck. It had taken him some time to realize that their deaths should not have eclipsed their lives. That he needed to remember them instead of burying them away, like forgotten pictures in the attic rafters.

"My brother was a daredevil, always reckless and wild,"

he recalled, smiling fondly as he thought about Harry. "He could never be still for long. He was forever riding, walking, hunting, engaging in some manner of sport. He was excellent at keeping wicket and a skilled footballer. I could never lay claim to one-fifth of his ability."

"Did you play cricket or football?" she asked, sounding genuinely curious.

"I played cricket incredibly poorly, I'm afraid. But I was reasonably skilled at rowing. Harry, however, was the recipient of most of the familial physical prowess."

Which had been why the knowledge that he had drowned had been so particularly painful for Alaric. How impossible it had been to fathom his vibrant, beloved brother, so strong and capable, helplessly meeting his end in the sea with their parents.

"What of your mother and father?"

"My mother was dreadful at cricket," he teased, trying to lighten the mood.

Lillian laughed softly, the sound husky and pleasant, even more so because he had been the source of her levity. "Is that so?"

"No. I'm lying, of course. She adored gowns and jewels and shopping. Perhaps a bit too much," he added wryly. "My father was congenial—he was happy if Mother was happy. Theirs was a love match, and he worshiped her until the end. She adored the Christmas season especially."

"Do you think she would have approved of me?" Lillian asked.

There was a hesitation in her voice that chipped away at the walls around his heart. This beautiful woman, so lauded in the newspapers, every detail of her wardrobe, appearance, and trousseau reported upon, this sought-after American heiress, had finally shown him a hint of vulnerability.

"I know she would have," he said. "And my father and

Harry as well. You are a perfect duchess, Lillian. You are elegant and refined, polite and intelligent, and kindhearted as well. Mrs. Greaves tells me you are already a favorite belowstairs."

His praise elicited a becoming pink flush on her cheeks. "You praise me far more than I deserve, I fear."

Over the course of the past few days, he had learned more about her, enough to know that she was not just a selfish, cossetted heiress as he had originally believed in the wake of discovering that bloody letter.

Alaric was going to have to tell her about discovering it. Soon. But for now, the words were not there. Or perhaps he didn't wish to find them and ruin this moment.

"I don't think I've praised you enough," he admitted.

She gave him a sidelong smile. "Well, if you insist, who am I to argue?"

Alaric chuckled, and they returned to their horses and spent the rest of the ride getting better acquainted, as they should have done months ago, before they had married. Before the letter had changed everything.

As his mother had been fond of saying, better late than never.

He could only hope his wife agreed.

CHAPTER 6

*L*illian and Alaric were seated in the drawing room before a roaring fire. The room was festooned with decorations, the scent of pine was in the air, and she found herself, for the first time, looking forward to Christmas. She would miss her parents, her friends, and the familiar. But perhaps she would forge new traditions with her husband.

Husband.

Already, the word held a different meaning now that Alaric was in residence. No longer poisonous. No longer strange. But a word that, perhaps, could be filled with promise, much like the festive season itself.

Tomorrow was Christmas Eve, and while she and Alaric had spent much time together, they still had yet to fully consummate their marriage. They had kissed. Shared stories of their childhoods. Spoken about what they liked to read, what they preferred to eat, about their hopes and dreams for their joined future. Alaric wanted children, including an heir to continue the ducal line. Lillian longed to be a mother as well, though she hadn't been certain how that would take shape, given the early weeks of their union.

But there was a renewed sense of promise in the air, giving her hope.

She had discovered that Alaric was an excellent singer, while she excelled at playing the piano. A charming sense of humor resided beneath his cool exterior. She had made a game of earning his smiles and laughs. His touch was gentle. His thoughts were complex. He was clever and witty, and she never wanted this little idyll at Wentworth Abbey to end, even though she knew it inevitably would.

Just as inevitable as her feelings for him were. Because she wasn't just falling in love with her husband. She had already done so. This newfound vulnerability frightened her, but there was no way for her to change it now.

They had spent many of their days making up for lost time, riding about the estate, Alaric showing her all the most-beloved corners of Wentworth Abbey, regaling her with tales of his contented youth. She felt very much as if he had given her a rare glimpse into the man he truly was, the one he had kept locked away from her behind a mask of polite indifference.

This evening, she had a sketchbook in hand and was working on a charcoal rendition of him as he sat on a chair, a book in hand. But it was no use. She frowned down at her work, thinking she couldn't manage to get the angle of his jaw just right, nor the handsome protrusion of his nose—such perfect symmetry and she could do his masculine beauty no justice.

"What has you looking so grim on this fine evening?" he asked.

Lillian glanced back in his direction to find his warm, brown stare upon her, searching. She had believed him quite engrossed in the volume he had chosen to read.

"I am despairing at my attempts to sketch you, if you must know," she admitted.

"You are sketching me?" He looked startled.

Her cheeks went warm. "I had intended to sketch the fire, but my eyes were drawn in a different direction. I decided to try to capture you, but I fear I lack the skill."

"Will you show me?"

She sighed, glancing back down at her efforts, which failed to capture the heat in his gaze, the riveting masculine beauty of his face. "Promise me you won't laugh."

"I would never laugh at your sketches," he said seriously. "I'm affronted you believe I would. Am I that dreadful?"

He had proven himself rather the opposite of dreadful, but Lillian still wasn't certain what to do with this new Wentworth. With *Alaric*.

"Of course not." Steeling herself, Lillian turned the sketchbook so that it faced him.

"Ah," he said slowly. "I see the problem."

"You do?"

"Yes, you haven't made my nose nearly long enough."

Lillian laughed. "But your nose isn't long."

"And you've made me look far too brooding and mysterious."

"But you *are* brooding and mysterious," she countered.

Indeed, so much of him remained a mystery that she dearly longed to unravel. More now than ever.

"What is so mysterious about me?" he asked, sounding curious.

"Everything."

He cocked his head at her. "In what way? I fear that to me, I am quite uninteresting and predictable."

She struggled to explain. "I feel as if I still don't know who you truly are. We have known each other for months, and yet I don't know much of you, aside from what you shared with me today."

"What else would you like to know?"

"What are you reading?" she asked, settling upon the easiest question.

"A volume of poetry by Elizabeth Barrett Browning."

"Not a book about sheep farming, then?"

He chuckled. "Should I be reading about sheep farming?"

"There were rather a lot of books on the subject in the library."

"I carry this particular volume along with me. You'll not find a great deal of poetry here at Wentworth Abbey, at least not on the shelves in the library."

"Why not?"

"Poetry was my mother's favorite. I had her books packed away when I began selling off the most valuable books in the libraries at my estates. I didn't want to risk any of them accidentally being sold or taken away."

Her heart gave a pang.

"Was the book you're reading one of hers?"

He nodded. "It seemed an excellent choice in present circumstances."

"Why?" she dared to ask, needing to know whether she was ascribing too much to his words.

"Because many of these poems are about emotions. They convey what it feels like to love."

"And how does it feel, love?"

"Love is an ache deep in one's soul, particularly when it is unreturned."

He spoke with the certitude of someone with experience.

"Have you loved before?" she found herself blurting.

She didn't want to know, and yet, she did.

Was Alaric in love with someone else? Perhaps he'd had a mistress and that had been the reason for his defection. He could have gone to Scotland to see her. Was his love for another woman the reason he'd yet to consummate their marriage? A flurry of questions rained down on her mind, her fingers gripping her sketchbook tightly.

"I have."

Lillian tried to strike down the disappointment that filled her like flood waters threatening to overwhelm. He'd never made a secret of his reasons for marrying her. What had she expected from him?

She swallowed down emotion. "Do you still love her?"

"Yes, I do." His gaze slipped to her mouth. "I think more now than ever before."

Why was he staring at her lips when he spoke of another?

Lillian's spine stiffened. "You needn't fear that I will be jealous. I have no illusions about our marriage and the reasons for it."

"But I think that perhaps you do, and I suspect it is also time for me to explain something that I should have seven months ago."

"Seven months ago?" Her brow furrowed. "When we became engaged?"

He rose from his chair and crossed the drawing room, seating himself at her side on the settee where she was perched. His scent washed over her, familiar and tempting. She watched as he gently took the sketchbook from her and laid it aside. He reached for her hands next, holding them in his.

"Do you remember when you asked me to kiss you after we signed the betrothal contract?" he asked.

And once more, heat rushed to her cheeks. It had been dreadfully forward of her then and the reminder now felt almost like a reproach. She was raw, her emotions bubbled up too closely to the surface, like a pot of boiling water on a stove.

"It was far too daring of me, and I shouldn't have done so."

"Yes, you should have. I was happy that you did." He gave her fingers a soft squeeze. "I'm still happy that you did so. But afterward, when you ran from me, I realized that some books had fallen to the floor. A letter had slipped from where it must have been tucked between the pages of one of them, and I picked it up."

Her heart sank, foreboding sweeping over her. The letter from Monsieur Dupont. She had hastily slipped it inside a book and forgotten its existence until now. The expression on her husband's face suggested that it was indeed the letter he had discovered.

"Did you read it?" she asked, dread making her stomach tense.

"It wasn't my intention to do so. But when I retrieved it from where it had fallen, a few words caught my eye. I realized it was a love letter of sorts, from a gentleman to you."

What a fool she had been.

"Alaric," she said urgently, "I can explain the letter."

"You needn't. What happened before we were married is the past."

"But I must," Lillian insisted, taking a deep breath before launching into her explanation. "The letter was from my painting instructor, Monsieur Dupont. When I first learned from my mother that I was expected to marry you, I was rebellious and angry. I foolishly wrote him to see if he had feelings for me, but I quickly learned that he didn't and that any interest he paid me was because I was Lillian Penrose and not because he truly cared." She paused, searching his gaze for censure and finding none. "It was a mistake, all of it."

"Do you still love him?"

She shook her head. "I never loved him. I know that now. But when I wrote to him, I was desperate. You and I were not yet engaged. I had only just met you for the first time and I was angry with my parents for arranging our courting and meeting without my permission. I was being rebellious, and then I..." Her words trailed off as realization hit her. "You said you found the letter after we kissed. Is that why you became so distant afterward, why you went to Scotland alone when we arrived in London? It wasn't just because you needed to meet with the architect my father had chosen, was it?"

"Yes, that is why I went alone," he admitted softly. "I thought you needed more time to adjust to the notion of marrying me whilst you had feelings for someone else. You were so miserable during the voyage, and then you seemed no happier after we disembarked in London."

Everything made sense. Alaric had believed she was brokenhearted over losing Monsieur Dupont and having to marry him instead. When in truth, she hadn't given her former painting instructor any thought at all in the months since her receipt of his letter. She had understood what a mistake it had been to suppose he was the answer she sought.

She was heartsick over the knowledge that Alaric had been keeping his discovery of the letter tucked away all this time. "Why did you not ask me?"

"How was I meant to ask you if you were in love with another man, Lillian?" His ordinarily composed façade cracked, showing her a glimpse of a man who was vulnerable yet again. "I suppose I was too damned afraid to hear the answer. My pride didn't want to know. If you were truly in love with someone else, I feared the confirmation would break me."

Lillian stared at him, astonished that he should care so much. That he had been so adept at hiding behind his formal, aristocratic mask. How had she failed to see the depth of feeling in her husband?

"I'm sorry about the letter," she said. "I never should have written him. I regret doing so, and if I'd had the slightest inkling that you had found his note to me, I would have explained."

"I couldn't bear the thought of you loving someone else, and I had no wish to force myself upon a wife who didn't want me," Alaric said.

She squeezed his fingers. "Surely you must know that wasn't the way of things. When you kissed me that day, everything changed. But then you simply carried on as if it had never happened, and I didn't know what to think. I thought that perhaps you had a mistress—"

"Never," he interrupted fervently. "I promised myself to you on the day we wed, and I will honor that vow, just as I will honor you, until the day I die."

Relief washed over her, followed quickly by confusion. "But if you don't have a mistress, then who are you in love with?"

"Can you not guess?" He brought her hand to his lips for an ardent kiss, his gaze growing intimate and tender. "You, Lillian. I'm in love with you. I fell in love during that first month during our courtship, and when I inadvertently saw that letter, it broke me."

"You…love me," she repeated, almost too afraid to believe it.

How could it be possible that the man she had married, the aloof stranger who had been so perfectly proper and polite for so much of their time together, was in love with her?

"I love you." He kissed her hand again. "I'm sorry I didn't tell you before, sorry I didn't ask about the letter. Sorry I abandoned you after we arrived in London. My God, I'm so sorry for everything, my darling Lillian. I couldn't have made a greater mess of this had I tried."

"You truly love me," she said again, awe overtaking her.

Suddenly, everything that had happened since that day in the study in New York came together with perfect clarity. All this time, she had supposed him incapable of feeling, when he had been carrying around the heavy weight of the belief she was in love with another. All this time, he had been in love with her.

"I truly do," Alaric said. "Pray forgive me for being hesitant to display my emotions. It has been difficult for me since the tragedy. I lost everyone I had ever loved that day, and it changed me forever."

Lillian swallowed against a rush of tears that threatened to fall. "You need not apologize to me, Alaric. I cannot begin to fathom how broken your heart must have been after you lost your family in such a terrible accident."

Knowing the depth of emotion that hid behind his stoic countenance was enough to make Lillian realize that she needed to be honest with her husband as well.

He gave her a look that was so tender, her heart ached at the sight. "You need not fear that I expect you to return my sentiments. I know you didn't want our marriage, that you didn't wish to marry a stranger your parents had selected solely for his title. I hope that given time, I can earn your love. I intend to do everything in my power to make that happen from this moment forward."

"You don't have to do anything to earn my love," she told him softly. "You already have it."

He stilled, his gaze intent upon hers. "I do?"

She took a deep breath, summoning the words her husband deserved to hear. "I love you, Alaric. Not anyone else. You. Always and forever you. My heart is yours."

He lowered his head, his lips finding hers, and they kissed. It was a sweet kiss, a consummation of all the suppressed love and desire that had been burning between them these last few months, kept at bay by their mutual fears. It was a revelation steeped in passion and unlocked secrets.

Lillian tugged her hands free so that she could touch him, finding his shoulders, absorbing his strength through her fingertips as she opened for his questing tongue. He tasted like plum pudding and Alaric, and nothing had ever been more delicious.

They kissed until they were both breathing hard, and he broke the kiss to caress her face with a gentle, reverent touch. "I do believe this is the best Christmas gift I've ever been given."

"If you must go to Scotland again, or to the end of the earth, take me with you," she said. "I want to be wherever you are."

"I'll never leave your side." He kissed the tip of her nose. "Happy Christmas, my love."

She blinked away the tears clouding her vision. "Happy Christmas, Alaric."

CHAPTER 7

Summoning her courage, Lillian knocked at the door joining her chamber to Alaric's. They had stayed in the drawing room by the fire, talking and kissing, until nearly midnight before withdrawing politely as they had done each night before to their respective chambers. She'd withdrawn to her room where her lady's maid had already had a bath awaiting her. Now, she was finished with her evening ablutions, her efficient servant dismissed for the evening.

The time had come to consummate their marriage.

All he had to do was answer her knock.

But silence reigned on the other side of the door and despite their earlier declarations of love and all those decadent kisses, Lillian began to fret. Was he already asleep? Did he not wish for company this evening?

Even worse, would he think she was being terribly forward by approaching his chamber in such a bold fashion?

The only way to know for certain was to knock again, so she did. Louder this time.

"Come," he called distantly.

And she heard something else, a faint splash of water. Hesitantly, she tried the latch, opening the door. She had not yet been inside his bedroom here at Wentworth Abbey, and for a moment, Lillian could do nothing but stare at the once-forbidden territory before her. A skitter of nervousness skipped down her spine. Seducing her husband was entirely new to her. She wasn't certain she knew what to do.

Her eyes found him as she hovered at the threshold. He was reclining in a large tub the servants must have brought up for him and bucketed full of steaming water from the kitchens as well. Unlike the mansion in New York she was accustomed to, the estate was still lost in some distant memory of the past. There hadn't been funds to install proper bathrooms with heated plumbing or electric lights before she had married Alaric, but they would soon begin restoring this estate, much like Fernross Castle.

"Lillian," he greeted her warmly, as if he weren't sitting naked in a tub of steaming water.

Her eyes affixed to his bare chest, which gleamed in the low light of the gas lamps. It was broad and muscled, his arms resting on the lip of the tub every bit as strong and well-delineated. She wetted her lips, which had suddenly gone dry, and forced her gaze back up to his.

"Alaric," she mumbled. "You're at your bath. I can come back later."

Her face was heating and so was her skin. Seeing him this way had reminded her of all the talks Mother had given Lillian before her wedding day. Three separate speeches, issued to varying degrees of mortification for Lillian. Mother had made what happens between a husband and wife sound like a dreaded chore.

You must hold still and think of something lovely, Lillian, she had urged me. *Let your husband do as he wishes. It will be over soon enough, and then you go to sleep.*

However, sleeping was the last thing she was thinking about as she took in the glistening, half-naked perfection of the man she had married.

"Don't go," he said, staying her when she was poised to flee. "I've finished bathing. Unless you'd care to join me?"

Unless she would care to...

Her eyes felt as if they may pop from her head as she stared at him, wondering if he had gone mad. "I'm wearing my night rail and dressing gown."

"You can remove them," he offered as calmly as if he had just commented upon a cloud in the sky instead of urging her to take off every stitch of clothing on her back.

And get into the bath with him.

Naked.

"I...I am fine as I am," she managed to stammer a bit breathlessly.

"Pity," he murmured, holding her stare.

Alaric was *flirting* with her. And he was also *naked*.

Naked, like he wanted her to be. Lillian's brain went numb, and she couldn't think of a single, coherent response. Her heart was pounding faster, and she felt an unfurling sensation inside her, a slow and steady ache she couldn't explain.

She had told herself she was well prepared for whatever the consummation of their marriage entailed. That, despite her mother's somewhat ominous warnings, she might find the act pleasant. She and Alaric were in love, after all. His kisses left her feeling flushed and yearning.

But when she had knocked at his door, she'd thought her husband would be...she didn't know...*dressed*. She'd thought he would be handsome Alaric, properly clothed in a dressing gown. Not bare-chested, charming, flirtatious, impossibly gorgeous, and *inviting her to join him in his bath*.

"I-I really should leave you to finish your bath," she spluttered. "I didn't mean to intrude."

"You could never intrude, my love," he told her softly, his dark eyes holding hers captive. "You're my wife."

There was something in his voice when he said those last two words that made her knees threaten to give in. Molten, liquid heat pooled between her thighs.

Before she could respond, he stood. No, that was not entirely accurate. He didn't merely stand. He rose from the tub like a god presiding over Mount Olympus. She was helpless to do anything but stare as water rushed in loving rivulets down his powerful body. He was a work of art. More beautiful than any marble sculpture. His musculature was on full display, from his taut abdomen to his strong arms.

Someone made a high-pitched sound that likely resembled a dying mouse, and to her everlasting shame, Lillian realized it was her.

She ought to look away. Give him some privacy.

But Lillian couldn't.

And when her gaze dipped lower, she was equally spellbound and shocked. Because a certain part of him was far larger than she had imagined, thick and long and rising stiffly toward her.

Oh my heavens.

How would what was meant to happen between them ever work? He was far too huge, surely.

Alaric said something, but she could scarcely hear him above the rushing in her ears.

"I beg your pardon?" she managed politely, as if she were not presently staring at his manhood, when, in fact, she was indeed gaping at his most secret place.

"I was wondering if you would mind handing me my towel," Alaric said, a smile in his voice.

Because he could plainly see her staring. *Dear God.* She

snapped her gaze to his face and shook her head, clearing the fog that had settled in her mind.

"Of course."

Lillian spied a towel folded on a low stool near the tub and forced herself across the room to fetch it for him. The aroma of his bath rose, musky and pleasant. She wondered if his bare skin would be similarly scented, and her heart pumped faster. When she handed him the towel, their fingers brushed.

She averted her gaze, sure her face was on fire.

"Thank you."

His voice was husky and low.

It was not just her face that was aflame. So was the rest of her. She had believed herself the bold one in knocking at his door, but Alaric was steadily proving her wrong. She didn't feel bold at all. She felt overwhelmed. Uncertain. As if butterflies had taken up residence in her stomach.

Maybe she was not as prepared for this after all, as she had believed herself to be.

"You can look at me now," he said, amusement in his voice.

Guiltily, Lillian jerked her gaze to him. He had wrapped the towel low around his hips, still leaving his glorious chest completely bare. His dark hair glinted in the light, and it looked as if he had combed it back from his forehead with his fingers.

"I *was* looking," she blurted and then instantly cursed herself inwardly for saying something so nonsensical and foolish.

Of course she had been looking. She had been ogling him.

He chuckled. "Do I make you uncomfortable, Lillian?"

"You aren't wearing any clothes."

"Shall I put some on, then?"

"No," she denied quickly. "I mean yes." Then she shook

her head. "You needn't on my account. I'm not accustomed to being in the presence of a man in *dishabille*, but you are my husband. I suppose I'll grow accustomed to it."

"Was there something you wished to speak with me about?" he asked gently.

A droplet of water was slowly gliding down the center of his chest.

She blinked. "Yes, there was. There is."

Stop looking at his chest, Lillian. Stop looking at his chest.

But she couldn't seem to help herself. Alaric's chest was quite intriguing. She was fascinated by the contrasts between the two of them. All the places where he was so hard and firm, so masculine and powerful, where she was soft and rounded, feminine and dainty in comparison.

"What was it that you wished to speak with me about?"

Lillian swallowed hard. "I wanted to know…"

The droplet traveled toward his navel, where there was a thin trail of dark hair that led lower and disappeared beneath the towel. His manhood remained stiff and large beneath the draped cloth, a noticeable protrusion.

"Yes?" he encouraged her in the same tone she imagined he might use for a small child who was newly learning to speak.

"I wanted to know if the time has come to consummate our marriage," she said in a rush, her cheeks scalding by the time she finished.

Everything changed. The air turned hot. She was hot. He was hot. They felt suddenly volcanic. Her nipples had tightened into points beneath her night rail. Anticipation and desire melted into one molten sensation low in her belly. Was she getting ill? Perhaps she was coming down with something. She was achy, and her skin felt too tight for her body.

She should return to her room. If she was taking sick, she really ought to go to bed.

Lillian didn't go anywhere, however. Instead, she stood rooted to the floor like a tree.

"I think it has," he told her at last. "If you're ready?"

It was as if he had read her mind. Everything within her was a maelstrom. She didn't think she would ever be fully ready for the emotions and sensations taking her by storm. She hadn't expected to feel so much. It was as if what she had believed was a tiny trickling stream had suddenly turned into an ocean. But it was too late to change her mind now, and she wasn't sure if she even wanted to because she loved this man.

She held his gaze. "Yes."

❄

LILLIAN LOVED HIM. It was more than Alaric had ever dared to yearn for. Before tonight, he had been hoping she was warming to him. And when she had said those precious words to him in the drawing room, he had been half-afraid he'd been merely dreaming and that he would wake to find her still eying him warily, as if he were a stranger she didn't dare trust. It hadn't been a dream, however.

But still, when he'd heard the knock at his door earlier, he had initially thought that he had imagined the sound. Until a second had come, perhaps more hesitant but no less persistent than the first.

Now, the lone-word response she gave him sent a sharp bolt of desire straight through him. For a moment, he could scarcely breathe. He hadn't expected to want her so much. Stone by stone, they had been dismantling each other's walls. It had begun that day with the Christmas decorations adorning the drawing room and had continued, ultimately leading them here, to this moment.

Alaric could tell she was nervous. For a woman so self-assured, Lillian had been flushing and tripping over her words from the moment she had spied him in the bath. But he had seen the way her eyes had clung lovingly to every bare inch of skin on him, and he knew why.

She wanted him.

This was new for her. He knew he had to proceed slowly. He didn't want to spook her.

"Give me your hand," he said softly.

Her brows snapped together. "My hand?"

He held his out, palm up. "It's located at the end of your arm, complete with five fingers."

She laughed, the honeyed sound slipping over him like a caress, and his cock hardened even more. "I know what a hand is."

"Then do it."

Hesitantly, she laid her palm flush against his. He brought it to his lips and kissed her knuckles, then guided her hand to his chest, laying it against his pounding heart.

Her lips parted, her eyes widening, pupils dilating.

"Do you feel that?" he asked.

She caught her bottom lip between her teeth and worried it before responding, "You...you aren't wearing a shirt."

God, she was utterly adorable, flustered like this. So ruffled and uncertain, bereft of her customary polish and perfection.

Why the hell had he waited so long to make her his? Why had he allowed that silly letter to come between them? He should have made love to her the very first night she'd been his wife. They wouldn't have spent this last month apart.

"I'm not," he agreed. "But that's not what I wanted you to feel."

"Oh? What, then?"

"My heart," he told her. "Do you feel how fast it thumps? I'm nervous, too."

"You don't feel nervous."

Alaric smiled at her. "How does nervous feel?"

"Hot all over," she whispered.

"That's not nervous." His head dipped toward hers. "That's desire."

He didn't wait for her response. He just settled his mouth over her soft, full lips. They had been kissing all week, but this kiss was different because it was the precursor to something more. Alaric reveled in the taste of her, sweet like the plum pudding they had enjoyed earlier for dessert—cinnamon, currants, and candied citrus. Her tongue eagerly moved against his.

They stayed thus for an indeterminate span of time, their lips moving as one, kissing each other senseless. The kiss deepened, growing carnal, and Lillian pressed herself more firmly against him, the crush of her breasts on his chest making his aching cock twitch. He could feel her body relaxing, melting into his. Soon, her hands were both moving, one settling on his shoulder and the other landing on his nape. Her fingers tangled in his wet hair, and he groaned into her mouth.

He hadn't expected to want her this much, with a need that threatened to tear him in two.

But their time together had been a careful dance, each step leading them closer to an inevitable finish.

He dragged his mouth from hers, intoxicated by her, and strung a path of kisses along her smooth jaw to her throat. He nuzzled the silken skin there, inhaling deeply of her jasmine scent. She shivered in his arms, her nipples hard buds grazing his bare chest. He opened his mouth and sucked on her flesh, gratified when she moaned in response.

"Alaric." She was breathless.

She was also still wearing her bloody dressing gown. Kissing to the hollow at the base of her throat, he set to work on the buttons running down the front of the prim garment. It was fashioned of a diaphanous fabric, and it had probably cost more than half his modest, outmoded wardrobe. But by the time he reached the tempting swells of her breasts, he lost his patience with the tiny shell disks and began tearing.

Buttons flew over the carpet with muffled thuds.

She said his name again, part outrage at his desecration of her evening attire, he had no doubt, but then she giggled like a girl. "You're ruining my dressing gown."

"Forgive me," he said.

Alaric was not truly apologetic, however. He would happily rip the blasted thing to shreds again in a second if it meant getting closer to her bare skin.

"You're forgiven." She smiled shyly up at him.

She was beautiful. Somehow, he managed to shove the dressing gown down her arms, only to realize that her night rail was also plagued by a thin row of buttons at the neck. Her breasts strained against the fine fabric, her nipples taunting him. He took her mouth with his to keep himself from tearing at this next impediment. Alaric was trying to be a gentleman. To proceed slowly. To woo her.

But it was difficult indeed. His wife's hands were moving over his body in a gentle, tentative exploration that felt impossibly good. He was an idiot for staying away so long, thinking to give her time to adjust to her new life, allowing his wounded heart and pride to keep him from her. For dithering in Scotland with that blasted architect. He should have been here at her side instead.

Where he belonged.

Their lips never leaving each other's for long, they somehow managed to strip away the layers separating them.

The bedclothes had been turned down earlier by an efficient chambermaid, rendering it easy for Alaric and Lillian to lie in his bed together, bereft of any coverings.

He moved from her mouth to sample all the soft, sweetly feminine skin he had unveiled. Her breasts were full and round, tipped with hard nipples. He cupped a breast in his hand tenderly, and she arched her back with a throaty murmur of encouragement. Dotting kisses over her skin, he moved to the peak of each breast, sucking lightly.

Her fingers tunneled through his hair, and she gasped. Alaric glanced up to find her watching him, her expression lax with desire. With her glorious flaxen hair unbound and spilling over his pillow, she was a far cry from the cool, refined heiress he had first met. Lillian was like a gemstone, so many different facets to her, and he had come to respect them all.

This particular one was just for him, however.

"Tell me if I go too fast, or if I do something you don't like, love," he said, wanting to please her more than he wanted to take his next breath.

"I...liked that very much," she said, giving him a coy smile.

"Excellent." He kissed the swell of her breast and then moved lower, staking his claim upon her supple curves. "Tell me if you want me to stop."

He knew she had likely never experienced anything like what he was about to do, but now that his lips were on her, he couldn't deny himself. He was ravenous, and nothing but more of his wife would do.

His kisses continued, and he insinuated himself between her legs, caressing as he worked his mouth over her hip bone. Her musky, feminine notes teased his senses. She stiffened as his lips ventured nearer to the juncture of her thighs.

"What are you..."

He kissed the top of her slit, then gently parted her folds and flicked his tongue over her clitoris.

"Oh!" she exclaimed, her hips jumping beneath him.

"Bringing you pleasure," he murmured, sparing her another glance, although it was difficult to take his eyes from her pretty pink pussy. "Did you like it?"

Burnished gold lashes swept over her eyes, hiding her thoughts from him for a moment before she answered, "Yes."

He returned his mouth to her, licking again and groaning at how wet she was. She tasted even better than plum pudding. Lost in her, he concentrated on the sounds she made, the way her body danced beneath him, alternating between sucking and teasing her with his tongue. When her release hit her, she cried out in abandon, bucking into his face. He stayed where he was, prolonging the pleasure for her, lapping at her, ridiculously pleased at how his reserved duchess had come apart for him.

But his cock couldn't take much more waiting. Gently, he teased a finger into her, trying to prepare her for him. He didn't want to cause her any pain or a moment of discomfort. The first kiss of her wetness on his fingertip spurred him on. He sank a finger into her tight heat to his knuckle. Then he waited a few heartbeats for her body to adjust, sucking hard on her swollen nub as he glided deeper. Her inner walls clenched him in a delicious grip, and he could already feel his cock leaking. He worked her into a new frenzy and didn't stop until she was coming again, clamping down on his finger as she rocked against him.

He pressed a wet kiss to her inner thigh and then dragged himself back up her body, gripping his cock and running it through her slippery folds to coat himself. With his other arm, he leveraged himself over her on the bed, an overwhelming rush of tenderness bursting inside his chest.

What a precious gift this woman was.

Somehow, they had found what they didn't know they were seeking in each other. It felt, in a word, *right*.

"Certain?" he asked her.

She pressed a hand to his cheek. "Certain. I'm yours, Alaric."

Her words spurred him on as if lightning had struck his very soul. He was electrified. He was also harder than marble as he guided his cock to her entrance and thrust. She was so wet and responsive, her pussy tightening on him and almost pushing him out. He kissed her throat and thrust deeper until he was fully seated. Their bodies were joined, breast to chest, hip to hip. Nothing could have prepared him for the intensity, the sheer pleasure.

Together, they moved, learning each other's bodies. Making love until they were both writhing together, poised on the precipice of something incredible. He took her mouth for another kiss as he sank deep, and she clamped down hard on him again, her tongue surging against his as her body bowed beneath him. Two more thrusts, and he emptied himself inside her, the force of his release unlike anything he had ever known.

In the aftermath, they held each other, their naked bodies spent and intertwined. He felt the steady beat of her heart, and hope for their future rose within him like the sun on Christmas morning.

EPILOGUE

CHRISTMAS EVE, TWO YEARS LATER

"Who invited my mother and father to join us for Christmas?" Lillian grumbled at Alaric good-naturedly as they watched her parents quibbling over which of them had gifted their daughter the best present and who should be able to hold her longer.

Presently, her father had her in his arms.

The drawing room had been filled with even more decorations than the previous two years combined, much to the delight of Mrs. Greaves. Lillian's mother and father had traveled across the Atlantic to spend the festive season with them, which, of course, meant that her mother had insisted upon helping with everything from the menus, to the color of the ribbons threaded through the tree, to the carols being sung. She had also had all of her favorite ornaments crated up and shipped along with them.

The Christmas tree could barely be seen.

"I do think that you are the one who invited them, my love," Alaric told her, placing a hand on the small of her back.

"Remind me never to do so again," she returned grimly, even as she leaned into his comforting presence at her side.

Almost three years ago, she had become engaged to a stranger. A handsome, proper English duke she hadn't wanted to marry.

Except an odd thing had happened their first Christmas together.

Somewhere between the candles, the mistletoe, and the plum pudding, they had finally lowered their mutual guards and confessed their love for each other. And now, they were happier than ever, along with their baby daughter, whom they had named after Alaric's mother, Victoria Jane.

"They seem happy enough," Alaric said, slanting a tender look in her direction. "Let them argue a bit longer and see if they come to blows before you endeavor to interrupt."

She laughed at his lighthearted teasing. "Who do you think will win their argument?"

He took her hand and brought it to his lips for a worshipful kiss. "If they are anything like the two of us, then your father will know better than to try to best her, for she is his superior in every way."

Lillian laughed again. "If I didn't know any better, Your Grace, I would think you are charming me in an attempt to get beneath my skirts."

"Don't say that too loudly," he warned with a roguish grin. "I would dearly hate to die of mortification just before Christmas Day, should either of your parents overhear." He paused, his smile deepening. "But was I successful?"

"I think you know you are always successful in that particular regard," she responded, her heart overflowing with love and contentment.

He winked. "I'm happy to hear it, wife. Merry Christmas, darling Lillian. I love you."

"I love you more," she told him. "Merry Christmas."

Across the drawing room, her mother appeared to win

the argument, and her father relinquished baby Victoria to her waiting arms.

All was right in their little world.

❄

THANK you so very much for reading *The Duke Under the Mistletoe*! I hope you enjoyed this heartwarming tale of a marriage of convenience gone right at the holiday season. If you love the decadence of a Victorian Christmas, be sure to check out my Christmas Dukes series, and read on for a sneak peek at book one, *The Duke Who Despised Christmas*.

Please stay in touch! The only way to be sure you'll know what's next from me is to sign up for my newsletter here: http://eepurl.com/dyJSar. Please join my reader group for early excerpts, cover reveals, and more here: https://www.facebook.com/groups/scarlettscottreaders. And if you're in the mood to chat all things steamy historical romance and read a different book together each month, join my book club, Dukes Do It Hotter right here: https://www.facebook.com/groups/hotdukes because we're having a whole lot of fun!

THE DUKE WHO
DESPISED CHRISTMAS

The Duke Who Despised Christmas
Chapter One

*S*omething was different at Blackwell Abbey this cold, gray winter's morning. The Duke of Sedgewick couldn't quite discern what it was, however.

Quint sniffed the air, a new, unfamiliar scent invading his nostrils. It smelled…verdant and crisp, with a slight tinge of sweetness. What the devil could it be? Whatever it was, he didn't bloody well like it.

"Dunreave!" His voice echoed in the marbled great hall like the lash of a whip cracking.

The servant who acted as both his butler and valet appeared, rather in the fashion of a wraith seeping from the old stone walls. "Your Grace?"

Dunreave was tall, though not as tall as Quint, and spare of form, with a solemn air that would have been more suited to a vicar than a domestic.

"What is that scent?" Quint demanded.

"Scent?" The man's dark brows furrowed in confusion.

"What scent, sir?"

He waved a gloved hand before him in irritation, indicating the air. "The smell in this damned great hall. Something has changed. What is it?"

Dunreave cleared his throat. "To the best of my knowledge, nothing has, Your Grace."

Quint ground his jaw. "The best of your knowledge isn't sufficient, Dunreave. Something has been changed. Discover what immediately, if you please."

"Yes, Your Grace."

"You know how I feel about change," he growled.

Dunreave winced. "Of course, Your Grace. I'll inquire about the scent with Mrs. Yorke at once."

The name—as unfamiliar as the smell—made Quint's eyes narrow. "Who the hell is Mrs. Yorke?"

"The new housekeeper, Your Grace."

That information gave him pause.

Quint stiffened. "I neither want, nor need, a housekeeper at Blackwell Abbey. I have no intention of entertaining visitors of any sort."

The last housekeeper hired by his mother—a Mrs. Brome, who had borne a perpetual scowl and rattled about everywhere with her nettlesome chatelaine—had been sent away several months ago, and the household had been delightfully quiet and absent of nuisances, such as an abundance of maids, ever since. The fewer people underfoot, the better. Quint didn't like people either.

"I am aware of how Your Grace feels about housekeepers," Dunreave said dutifully.

"Then why is she here?" he snapped impatiently before giving the air another sniff.

Was the scent *her*, the unwanted housekeeper, then? If so, he'd toss her out of Blackwell Abbey himself.

Dunreave looked as if he had just swallowed a fish bone

and presently had it lodged in his throat. "The dowager duchess selected her for the situation, Your Grace."

Curse his mother. Why did she insist upon interfering? He had banished her from Blackwell Abbey, and yet she continued to meddle from afar.

"There is no situation, because I *don't want a bloody housekeeper*." He was shouting by the time he finished, which he regretted.

It wasn't Dunreave's fault that Quint's mother was as stubborn as a dog who had scented his favorite pig trotter hidden in the dirt and refused to surrender until he had dug it free of the earth. In this case, Quint was the pig trotter. However, he wished to remain quite miserably buried in a tomb of his own making.

Dunreave winced again, pushing his spectacles up the bridge of his nose. "I will write the dowager duchess to inform her, Your Grace."

Quint no longer had a wife, and the distinction of referring to his mother as the dowager duchess was unnecessary. A reminder of what he lost. And yet, his mother and the domestics had grown accustomed to the change when he had married Amelia.

"I'll write her myself," he snarled, the weight of guilt and the pain of grief pressing down on his chest like a boulder, omnipresent particularly at this time of year. "But this Mrs. Yates must go."

"Mrs. Yorke, Your Grace," Dunreave corrected.

Quint's lip curled. "I don't give a damn what her name is. I just want her gone forthwith."

"Of course, sir." Dunreave bowed. "I'll find Mrs. Yorke and tell her she is dismissed at once."

"Yes. Do that."

Feeling like a churl and yet helpless to stop the frustration burning through his mangled hide, Quint decided against the ride he had planned for this morning. Instead, he spun on his heel and stalked toward the drawing room, determined to find the source of the scent.

By God, if only his mother would allow him to wallow in the countryside in peace. Bad enough that she sent him an endless string of letters exhorting him to join her in London or to accompany her to country house parties or Christ knew what societal nonsense she had deemed a proper lure. This was the third housekeeper she had sent him in the span of six months.

He stopped near the broken fountain hidden in an alcove just behind the great hall when he heard a strange sound—the tinkling of water sluicing and trickling merrily down. But no, that couldn't be. The fountain was broken.

Quint stalked into the alcove, shocked to discover that the ornate, carved fish that decorated the massive fountain were indeed spitting water, just as they had been designed to do a century earlier.

He hadn't ordered the fountain's repair.

When had it been done? And without his knowledge?

Clenching his jaw, he left the alcove, following the familiar path to the drawing room. With each step, the scent grew stronger. Until he had reached the open door and made a more astonishing discovery still.

Greenery.

Everywhere.

It festooned the mantel, hung suspended over the heavy old curtains, and in two corners of the drawing room stood not one, but *two* trees, ornamented with candles and shining trinkets and baubles.

He had finally discovered the source of the scent.

Not only had someone repaired his fountain without his

consent. They had also decorated his goddamn drawing room.

"Dunreave!" he roared.

Want more? Get *The Duke Who Despised Christmas* now.

DON'T MISS SCARLETT'S OTHER ROMANCES!

Complete Book List
HISTORICAL ROMANCE

Heart's Temptation
A Mad Passion (Book One)
Rebel Love (Book Two)
Reckless Need (Book Three)
Sweet Scandal (Book Four)
Restless Rake (Book Five)
Darling Duke (Book Six)
The Night Before Scandal (Book Seven)

Wicked Husbands
Her Errant Earl (Book One)
Her Lovestruck Lord (Book Two)
Her Reformed Rake (Book Three)
Her Deceptive Duke (Book Four)
Her Missing Marquess (Book Five)
Her Virtuous Viscount (Book Six)

DON'T MISS SCARLETT'S OTHER ROMANCES!

Wicked Dukes Society
Duke with a Reputation (Book One)
Duke with a Debt (Book Two)
Duke with a Secret (Book Three)
Duke with a Lie (Book Four)
Duke with a Duchess (Book Five)

Christmas Dukes
The Duke Who Despised Christmas (Book One)
The Duke Who Ruined Christmas (Book Two)

League of Dukes
Nobody's Duke (Book One)
Heartless Duke (Book Two)
Dangerous Duke (Book Three)
Shameless Duke (Book Four)
Scandalous Duke (Book Five)
Fearless Duke (Book Six)

Notorious Ladies of London
Lady Ruthless (Book One)
Lady Wallflower (Book Two)
Lady Reckless (Book Three)
Lady Wicked (Book Four)
Lady Lawless (Book Five)
Lady Brazen (Book 6)

Unexpected Lords
The Detective Duke (Book One)
The Playboy Peer (Book Two)
The Millionaire Marquess (Book Three)
The Goodbye Governess (Book Four)

Dukes Most Wanted

DON'T MISS SCARLETT'S OTHER ROMANCES!

Forever Her Duke (Book One)
Forever Her Marquess (Book Two)
Forever Her Rake (Book Three)
Forever Her Earl (Book Four)
Forever Her Viscount (Book Five)
Forever Her Scot (Book Six)

The Wicked Winters
Wicked in Winter (Book One)
Wedded in Winter (Book Two)
Wanton in Winter (Book Three)
Wishes in Winter (Book 3.5)
Willful in Winter (Book Four)
Wagered in Winter (Book Five)
Wild in Winter (Book Six)
Wooed in Winter (Book Seven)
Winter's Wallflower (Book Eight)
Winter's Woman (Book Nine)
Winter's Whispers (Book Ten)
Winter's Waltz (Book Eleven)
Winter's Widow (Book Twelve)
Winter's Warrior (Book Thirteen)
A Merry Wicked Winter (Book Fourteen)

The Sinful Suttons
Sutton's Spinster (Book One)
Sutton's Sins (Book Two)
Sutton's Surrender (Book Three)
Sutton's Seduction (Book Four)
Sutton's Scoundrel (Book Five)
Sutton's Scandal (Book Six)
Sutton's Secrets (Book Seven)

Rogue's Guild

DON'T MISS SCARLETT'S OTHER ROMANCES!

Her Ruthless Duke (Book One)
Her Dangerous Beast (Book Two)
Her Wicked Rogue (Book 3)

Royals and Renegades
How to Love a Dangerous Rogue (Book One)
How to Tame a Dissolute Prince (Book Two)

Sins and Scoundrels
Duke of Depravity
Prince of Persuasion
Marquess of Mayhem
Sarah
Earl of Every Sin
Duke of Debauchery
Viscount of Villainy

With *NYT* Bestselling Author Melanie Moreland
Maid for the Marquess

Sins and Scoundrels Box Set Collections
Volume 1
Volume 2

The Wicked Winters Box Set Collections
Collection 1
Collection 2
Collection 3
Collection 4

Wicked Husbands Box Set Collections
Volume 1
Volume 2

Notorious Ladies of London Box Set Collections
Volume 1
Volume 2

The Sinful Suttons Box Set Collections
Volume 1
Volume 2

Stand-alone Novella
Lord of Pirates
The Duke Under the Mistletoe

CONTEMPORARY ROMANCE
Love's Second Chance
Reprieve (Book One)
Perfect Persuasion (Book Two)
Win My Love (Book Three)

Coastal Heat
Loved Up (Book One)

Writing as Lora Whitney

Mafia Romance
Andriani Brothers
Brutal Devil (Book One)
Cruel Sinner (Book Two)

ABOUT THE AUTHOR

USA Today and Amazon bestselling author Scarlett Scott™ writes steamy Victorian and Regency romance with strong, intelligent heroines and sexy alpha heroes. She lives in Pennsylvania and Maryland with her Canadian husband, their adorable identical twins, a demanding diva of a dog, and a zany cat who showed up one summer and never left.

A self-professed literary junkie and nerd, she loves reading anything, but especially romance novels and poetry. Catch up with her on her website https://scarlettscottauthor.com. Hearing from readers never fails to make her day.

Scarlett's complete book list and information about upcoming releases can be found at https://scarlettscottauthor.com.

Connect with Scarlett! You can find her here:
Join Scarlett Scott's reader group on Facebook for early excerpts, giveaways, and a whole lot of fun!
Sign up for her newsletter here
https://www.tiktok.com/@authorscarlettscott

- facebook.com/AuthorScarlettScott
- x.com/scarscoromance
- instagram.com/scarlettscottauthor
- bookbub.com/authors/scarlett-scott
- amazon.com/Scarlett-Scott/e/B004NW8N2I
- pinterest.com/scarlettscott

Made in United States
Orlando, FL
16 December 2025